Searching for Mine

Also from Jennifer Probst

The Billionaire Builders
Everywhere and Every Way

Searching for Series
Searching for Someday
Searching for Perfect
Searching for Beautiful
Searching for Always
Searching for You

The Marriage to a Billionaire series
The Marriage Bargain
The Marriage Trap
The Marriage Mistake
The Marriage Merger
The Books of Spells

Executive Seduction

All the Way

The Sex on the Beach Series
Beyond Me
Chasing Me

The Hot in the Hamptons Series
Summer Sins

The Steele Brother Series
Catch Me
Play Me
Dare Me
Beg Me

Dante's Fire

Searching for Mine

A Searching For Novella

By Jennifer Probst

1001 Dark Nights

EVIL EYE
CONCEPTS

Searching for Mine
A Searching For Novella
By Jennifer Probst

1001 Dark Nights

Copyright 2016 Triple J Publishing Inc
Print ISBN: 978-1-942299-23-3

Foreword: Copyright 2014 M. J. Rose

Published by Evil Eye Concepts, Incorporated

Acknowledgments

Ah, so many people to thank!

Smooches to the amazing 1001 Dark Nights team – Liz Berry and M.J. Rose. I'm so honored to be asked to participate in this series, and humbled to stand beside my talented fellow authors. I love this world you created!

Special shout-out to my street team, The Probst Posse. You guys helped me create Connor's story and it was a beautiful team effort. I love brainstorming with you guys! Here's a few specific names to thank for their specific suggestions I incorporated into the book!

Marlene Brown, Elizabeth Clinton, Stephanie Flowers Newman, Maybelline Smith, Katherine Thompson Allen, Tina Hobbs and Ada Frost

One Thousand And One Dark Nights

Once upon a time, in the future…

*I was a student fascinated with stories and learning.
I studied philosophy, poetry, history, the occult, and
the art and science of love and magic. I had a vast
library at my father's home and collected thousands
of volumes of fantastic tales.*

*I learned all about ancient races and bygone
times. About myths and legends and dreams of all
people through the millennium. And the more I read
the stronger my imagination grew until I discovered
that I was able to travel into the stories… to actually
become part of them.*

*I wish I could say that I listened to my teacher
and respected my gift, as I ought to have. If I had, I
would not be telling you this tale now.
But I was foolhardy and confused, showing off
with bravery.*

*One afternoon, curious about the myth of the
Arabian Nights, I traveled back to ancient Persia to
see for myself if it was true that every day Shahryar
(Persian: شهريار, "king") married a new virgin, and then
sent yesterday's wife to be beheaded. It was written
and I had read, that by the time he met Scheherazade,
the vizier's daughter, he'd killed one thousand
women.*

*Something went wrong with my efforts. I arrived
in the midst of the story and somehow exchanged
places with Scheherazade — a phenomena that had
never occurred before and that still to this day, I
cannot explain.*

*Now I am trapped in that ancient past. I have
taken on Scheherazade's life and the only way I can
protect myself and stay alive is to do what she did to
protect herself and stay alive.*

*Every night the King calls for me and listens as I spin tales.
And when the evening ends and dawn breaks, I stop at a
point that leaves him breathless and yearning for more.
And so the King spares my life for one more day, so that
he might hear the rest of my dark tale.*

*As soon as I finish a story... I begin a new
one... like the one that you, dear reader, have before
you now.*

Chapter One

"A woman must have money and a room of her own if she is to write fiction"—
Virginia Woolf

Connor Adam Dunkle stared at the paper. The circled letter mocked
him in bright red, and with a false merriness that his professor
probably relished.

A big fat F.

Impossible.

His gaze scanned the bleeding type scrawl filled with unknown
marks, initials, and cross outs. At the end, two sentences were written
in elegant cursive they didn't teach in school any longer.

*Deduction of two letter grades for lateness. Overall, a poorly thought, shallow
type paper with nothing to back up the opinion via the text.*

Connor Dunkle studied the woman who was his last obstacle
blocking him from getting his needed degree.

Professor Ella Blake.

If he'd ever created an image of a spinster librarian, this woman
would have been his inspiration. From her drab, baggy fitting clothes,
to the black glasses hiding most of her features, she practically faded
into the background. Her hair was twisted up into a tight bun, giving
her face a bit of a pinched look. Her gray sweater and black trousers
did nothing for her figure, or her skin tone. The only brightness in her
entire collage was a slash of red-orange lipstick, which became so
garish with her olive skin, it literally made an onlooker jerk back.

"Many of you disappointed me with your papers. I suggest better preparation is in order to pass this class. Our first exam is Friday and there will be another paper due shortly. Please make sure you refer to the syllabus for due dates. I do not appreciate or reward lateness."

Did she shoot him a look or was that his imagination?

Unbelievable. He'd deliberately approached her last week and explained his grueling schedule. With his demanding workload and ambitious course work, he'd specifically asked Professor Blake for an extension on the paper.

Hadn't she agreed?

It had taken him a lot to register for college at thirty-eight years old, but he had his eye on a management position at Bilkins Construction, and he was determined to change his life. He'd taken extra courses and jammed in a four-year degree into two. Finally, graduation loomed before him, but he'd put off fulfilling his last course requirement of Composition 102. Of course, now he ended up with a sexually frustrated teacher focused on feminist literature to make excuses for her own lack of a love life.

"We'll be diving more into short stories and examining the female writer and what she brought to society in comparison to men at the time. I'd like to hear thoughts on *The Yellow Wallpaper*. What do you think made the story so popular? What was the writer really trying to tell us?"

Connor hid a bored sigh and tuned out of the discussion. He'd fix it. He'd be extra nice and charming and give her some needed male attention. Maybe she'd forgotten, and he'd just remind her, they'd laugh about it, and he'd get a damn C.

Professor Blake paced the front of the room in her usual black boots that made no sound. He wondered if she ever wore stilettos. Probably didn't know what they were. She preferred shoes with no sex appeal, no heel, and no sense of fun. What type of underwear did she wear to match those awful outfits? Probably cotton. Maybe even granny panties in plain white.

"Mr. Dunkle?"

His head shot up in pure surprise. She was staring at him with a focused expression that almost made him blush. Almost. Of course, she had no clue he'd been wondering about the look of her panties. He gave her an easy grin that usually charmed women within a few seconds. "Yes?"

"I'm interested in your opinion of the story."

Shit. He hadn't understood the end. Hell, he hadn't understood much of it and daydreaming in class wasn't helping him. He kept the grin and nodded. "I thought it was a brave way of portraying the character."

There. Sounded good. She tapped her finger against her orange-red lips and leaned against the side of the desk. "Interesting. Tell me more."

Shit.

He tried not to sweat and frowned, as if thinking hard, and tried to buy time. "Well, the writer struggled with identity."

Connor had heard that line in many classes and felt it was a solid portrayal of the ridiculous story he'd hated. He waited for her to move on to someone else, but instead she actually walked up the aisle to his seat. Sweat pricked his forehead. He hadn't felt this put on the spot since high school.

"So, the writer was brave and struggled with identity. Why don't you tell me exactly what you feel the story is about?"

And that's when Connor realized she knew. Up close, her dull brown eyes glinted with flecks of gold-green, pulling an observer in. Her face seemed expressionless but Connor caught the challenge in her gaze—the knowledge he had no clue what he was talking about, and she was going in for the kill.

Who would've thought a drab English professor could be so ruthless?

He regrouped and assessed the situation. Tilting his head, he stared right back, refusing to back down. "I think the story was ridiculous and contrived. It was a big whine fest of a character trapped in a room, obsessed with the wallpaper but not enough guts to get herself out of the situation. That's what I thought about the story."

The class tittered. He waited for her attack, knowing he'd challenged her in class, which was her natural terrain. Still, Connor didn't care. That story sucked and it was a relief to admit it.

A small smile touched her lips. "A fair and honest assessment," she concluded.

He grinned.

"By a reader who has no idea what he's reading. By a reader who has no desire to try and follow the writer or do more than lazily lay back and wait for the car wrecks, or sex scene, or shootout. We've become a society who wants so badly to be entertained, without using a brain cell, and refuses to do the work to engage and follow greatness. Frankly, Mr. Dunkle, you disappoint me. I had expected much more of you."

His grin disappeared.

She walked away on soundless shoes and pointed to the blackboard. "Maybe we can salvage it for the rest of the class. Let's begin."

Connor held back a groan.

This was going to be a bitch of a semester.

Chapter Two

"I thought how unpleasant it is to be locked out; and I thought how it is worse, perhaps, to be locked in"—*Virginia Woolf*

Ella watched her students file out of class but her attention was focused on one particular individual.

Connor Dunkle.

She sensed a play coming on, and she was actually going to enjoy it. Teaching provided her a sick sense of satisfaction when she got to take an egotist, smug person and knock them down a few notches. It also offered a perfect conduit to change the thinking and view of the world one student at a time. Sure, sometimes she felt as if she made no difference with her classes. But once in a while, she lasered in on a student who needed to be challenged.

"Professor Blake? Can I talk to you a moment?"

She turned, and right on cue, there he was. Ella hid her smile and wondered how the first round would fare. She'd pegged him from the first day, but sometimes a student surprised her.

"Yes, Mr. Dunkle?" She peered over her thick-framed glasses. She could've picked trendy or delicate frames, but she liked the way these intimidated her students. "What can I do for you?"

His charming grin could've short-circuited the light bulbs or rendered one speechless. Had she ever seen such perfect white teeth? The man was a walking delectable treat for the female vision, but Ella had prepared. She checked in with her body and was quite pleased. Other than a recognizable hum between her thighs, she was completely in control. Of course, he didn't know that. Ella judged there weren't many offers Connor made that were turned down. The reason was all six foot five inches that towered over her desk with lean, cut muscles evident beneath his casual clothes. Dirty blond hair lay messily over his brow. He wore it long, and the thick strands curled around the edge of his ears. His face was sculpted quite beautifully, from the high cheekbones, full lips, and perfect dimples. He reminded her briefly of a young Robert Redford from her favorite movie, *The Way We Were.* Sure, Redford was old now, but Ella believed the greats like Newman and Redford and Brando paved the way for Pitt and Hemsworth. And damned if her fingers didn't itch just once to brush those gold streaked strands from his forehead.

His eyes delivered the final one-two punch. Crystal blue swirled with a touch of green, clear as glass and deep as the sea. Eyes like that could mesmerize prey, but Ella had tons of practice restraining messy desires. She met his gaze, ignoring the tiny tumble in her belly, and kept her gaze on the prize.

"Yes?" she asked with a bit of impatience. He blinked, somewhat confused she hadn't ducked her head or stuttered. Oh, this one needed a reality check. Had he ever been rejected? Or was he one of the lucky ones who slid through life unscathed by others? Huh. Another similarity to Redford's character. She was going to have to re-rent that movie again.

"I think there was a misunderstanding," he began. His body language reeked of open friendliness with just a touch of sex. His navy blue T-shirt stretched tight across his chest, and his jeans were worn low on his hips, which were now cocked in a very appealing angle. He tilted his head to ensure intimacy, and damned if his dimples hadn't popped out. Oh, he was good.

He held out the paper. "I got an F. I apologize again for turning it in late. See, I'm about to graduate with a business management degree. I need to pass this course." His smile held well. "When we last spoke, I assumed you understood my position and told me it was acceptable to turn it in a few days late."

Oh, she remembered that conversation perfectly. He'd given her excuse after excuse for why he deserved more time, and she just nodded and didn't have to say a word. The man was probably so used to women giving him everything he wanted, he hadn't even bothered to wait for her verbal assent. Just walked away with a smile and a wink. He'd actually winked at her like this was 1970 and calling women in authority by *honey* and *babe* was fine.

"It was acceptable," she said calmly. "But if you'd read your syllabus carefully, you'd see each day it comes in late one full letter grade is taken off. I gave you a break though, Mr. Dunkle. I didn't count the weekend because I was feeling quite generous. Is that it?"

He blinked. Confusion flickered over his face and she had to tamp down a chuckle. He leaned in just a few inches and dropped his voice to a concerned level. "Professor Blake, I need to get a C in this class. My job right now depends on my graduation this June."

Her eyes glinted behind her glasses with pure intention. "Did you read *The Story of an Hour* by Kate Chopin? Or did you scan the Internet for analysis and summaries and stick them into your paper to make it look like you read it?"

Oh, she knew that look well. Ella waited to see if he'd lie straight to her face. A tiny crease in his brow gave him away. She was the one surprised when he finally answered. "No."

"No, what, Mr. Dunkle?"

"No, I didn't read the story. I tried. But I got bored and stopped."

She nodded. "I'd suggest if you want to pass my class you begin taking it seriously and doing the assignments. On time."

His aura simmered with frustration. "I understand. I'll be sure to read the next short stories thoroughly. Who's the next author we're studying?"

"Virginia Woolf."

He looked like he'd rather stick needles in his eye than read Woolf, but she gave him credit. He kept his expression open and understanding. "Fascinating. Hey, maybe we can get some coffee after class? Discuss some of your viewpoints. Get to know one another better? I feel like we may have gotten off on the wrong foot."

Unbelievable. The man just kept digging the crater larger and larger. He'd be lucky to graduate. She switched to her disapproving teacher voice: hard, controlled, and full of ice. "I dislike clichés, Mr. Dunkle. In both speech and company."

"Huh?"

"Gotten off on the wrong foot," she pointed out. "It's called a cliché. Look it up. Now, do you have any issues regarding the next assignment?"

He cleared his throat. "I'm just surprised we're reading another woman writer. This was never explained as a feminist course. I assumed we'd be reading Hemmingway, or Fitzgerald, or Poe. Getting more of the male perspective in society, too, you know?"

Once again, he realized he'd misspoken too late. Her gaze flicked over him, then slid away in dismissal.

"You know what they say about the word assume, Mr. Dunkle?"

"No."

Her smile was mean. "It makes an ASS out of you and me. Now if you'll excuse me, I need to get ready for my next class."

She focused on the stack of papers in front of her and began to read. His stunned silence seethed with unspoken emotions, but finally he walked away with his failing paper clutched in his hand. She risked a peek.

His stride owned pure grace and swagger. His tight, perfect ass made women want to weep. Or cop a feel.

She tamped down the flare of guilt from ogling a student, but the man was her age and ready to graduate, so it wasn't all that terrible. Besides, she'd never date the man. If he thought their little chat meant she was going to forgive lateness or inane answers in her class, Connor Dunkle would learn quickly enough.

Sighing, she began prepping for her next class. God, she was tired. She loved teaching, but lately, burnout threatened. How long had it been since she spent a night out? Or did anything more exciting than grading papers and playing Wii U Super Smash Brothers? She adored her ten-year-old son, but maybe she needed more balance in her life. Ella didn't want Luke growing up thinking women didn't leave the house other than to work. But every time she thought about going out with some friends for a drink, mama guilt kicked in. They'd already been forced to move twice before she got her permanent job at Verily College, and he was still adjusting to a new neighborhood and school. How could she leave him to pursue her own fun? The divorce may have been final for a year now, but the first year was filled with pain, anger, and lawyers back and forth. Luke probably needed more time to accept his parents would never get back together. He'd probably freak at the idea of her trying to date, and Lord knows her first priority was to her son.

Ella sighed. She had no time for dating anyway. Weekends were filled with endless errands and running around. The idea of putting on something more than a pair of sweats seemed painful.

Right now, her legs resembled a porcupine. If she ever had sex again, she'd need to bribe the beautician to give her a bikini wax.

She was thirty-five years old, and an official old maid. Maybe they'd make a card in her honor one day. If children even played that game anymore. Oh, Lord, now her mind was chattering about inane things again and she needed to get herself together.

Ella bet Connor didn't have such problems. His biggest issue was probably what woman to sleep with and what type of beer to drink with dinner. Yeah, she was being judgy, but damned if she didn't feel like she had the right just this once.

She sorted folders and her fingers closed around the glossy postcard she'd found in the Verily bakery. With purple and silvery scroll, the logo of Kinnections matchmaking agency made her pause. Tapping her finger against the edge, she rotated it in her hands and pondered.

It may be a bit pricey, but imagine someone taking the time to personally screen her matches? No bars or losers or meat markets to deal with. No dreaded Internet. Maybe there'd be a nice single father out there who was perfect for her. A man who took responsibility seriously. A man who wouldn't dump his family for a newer, flashier model like her dickhead ex-husband.

The next group of students came straggling in, and Ella shoved the card back into the pile of papers. She'd think about it. Right now, she needed to concentrate on Edith Wharton.

Ella got back to work.

Chapter Three

"I would always rather be happy than dignified."—*Charlotte Brontë, Jane Eyre*

Connor climbed the steps to his apartment, looking forward to some good TV, his meatball parm sub, and a cold Guinness with the perfect head. The conversation with Professor Blake kept replaying over and over in his head. What had he done wrong? The damn class was ruining his perfect GPA, which he'd worked hard for. Was she really going to bust his balls on essays that meant nothing?

He muttered a few choice curse words and stopped short. A voice hit his ears along with the sound of metal dragging on concrete.

"What's a matter, new boy? You too good to hang with us? Maybe I'll teach you a lesson. Gimme that DS!"

"No! Leave me alone!"

Connor bit back a groan and turned. The same three boys—he called them the gangsters—were tormenting some poor kid who had been shoved to the ground and pinned by his bike. An open backpack spilled a variety of contents over the sidewalk. The main bully gave a satisfied sneer and held the red Nintendo DS high over his head.

Little shits. They liked to play dirty and tended to pick out kids a few years younger. Connor knew the type well. His younger brother, Nate, had fallen victim to bullying in school and it had almost destroyed his ability to concentrate on his studies. Connor made sure no one messed with him, but he felt bad for the kids who had no one to protect them.

Connor put his purchases down and walked over to the crew.

"Practicing for prison?" he drawled. He stood in front of them with his arms crossed casually, an intimidating stare on his face. Like clockwork, the three of them looked at each other, their faces reflecting wariness and a coward's fear. Yeah, the bullies were only strong together. Break them up and they were helpless. "Here. Let me help you."

The boy on the ground ignored his outstretched hand and dragged himself to his feet. No tears shone in his dark eyes, but his skin was mottled red, and his lower lip trembled slightly. Still, pure rebellion reflected in his face and attitude. His dark hair was cut too short, emphasizing a wicked cowlick in the front, and he was skinny and all legs. A thin trickle of blood dripped down his arm. Probably a scraped elbow. He wore a red sweatshirt with the Captain America logo, athletic pants, and some type of expensive looking sneakers. Connor respected him wanting to handle the situation himself, especially at his age. What was he, about nine? Ten?

"We weren't doing nothing," the lead gangster replied. "He fell off his bike."

The boy didn't deny it. He stared at the bullies with a fierce resentment that shimmered in the air. His hands clenched into tight fists, but he didn't move, just shifted back and forth on his feet.

"Convenient. Give me the DS."

"It's mine!" lead gangster whined.

Connor looked at the kid but he didn't claim the DS. Keeping a stubborn silence, he met the gangster's gaze and refused to back down.

Connor shook his head. "Tough. I'm claiming the DS. I've been dying to try out some games so it's now mine."

The boys looked at him as if he'd gone nuts, and Connor used their shock to smoothly snatch the DS from the bully's hand. "You can't do that!" the second gangster cried. "That's stealing."

"Guess I'll be sharing a jail cell with you one day, huh? Listen up. Next time you think you're gonna have a bit of fun at some younger kid's expense, remember this. I can find each of you alone and make you regret it. Got it?"

The leader stepped back. "Whatever. Come on, guys. Let's get out of here."

They trudged away in their ragtag group. Connor picked up the bike from the ground and thrust out the DS. "Here you go. No thanks necessary, kid."

"I didn't need your help," the boy hissed in fury. Connor jerked back at the frustration glinting from his brown eyes. "I had it handled. You screwed up everything, dude! Now they're gonna be looking for me cause they think I'm a wuss!"

Connor blinked. "Are you kidding me? You would've gotten beat up. I've seen those kids around and they don't play nice. Trust me, they won't mess with you anymore."

The boy yanked back the DS and his bike, shoving his backpack over his arm. "Whatever."

Connor rolled his eyes. "When did that word make a comeback? I mean, really?"

The kid didn't answer, just shook his head and dragged his bike toward the building next door. Huh. Guess he was a new neighbor. Connor hadn't seen any moving trucks, but he hoped the grumpy old man was finally gone. Anyone was better than a grizzled man who sat on the front stoop and bellowed at strangers on the street, drinking cheap whiskey from a brown paper bag. Even a surly kid.

Connor watched the red door shut and turned back to his own place. Maybe he should knock on the door this weekend and introduce himself. The neighborhood wasn't the best, but the location was prime for commuting to Manhattan and keeping rents low. Other than the band of bullies who haunted the streets, there weren't drugs or gangs. Just a bunch of older stone buildings with ancient plumbing, leaky windows, and pothole-ridden streets.

Still worked for him.

Connor trudged inside and reheated his dinner. The interior of his apartment didn't reflect the shabby exterior. He'd updated the original dull beige walls and carpet with a rich blue, and his brother's girlfriend, Kennedy, had transformed the bachelor pad into a home using a few feminine touches to brighten up the place. He'd moved from his old apartment he'd shared with Nate to save money, ignoring his brother's protests that he'd cover his expenses until Connor finished school.

Hell, no.

Connor had spent his life taking care of his little brother and raising him. Though Nate was now a fancy rocket scientist who used to work for NASA, Connor refused to take his charity. But he hadn't been able to afford the tuition so they'd struck a deal. Since Connor had worked three jobs to get Nate through college when he was young, Nate would front his tuition bill. Connor could live with that, knowing he'd pay back his brother every dime once he got into a management position. He'd quickly moved to this apartment to save on rent and was now able to live comfortably.

He may not have fancy granite counters or stainless steel appliances, but everything worked, including the big screen TV. The furniture was secondhand, but it was solid wood mahogany, with clean, masculine lines. The extra bedroom was a nice perk, so he used it for his workout equipment and skipped the gym membership. Photos of architectural buildings and bridges filled the walls, bringing a sense of wonder and creativity to the space. His textbooks stuffed the antique bookcase, and he'd created a small workspace in the corner of the living room, saving a spot for where he'd hang his degree.

He pulled out his sub, cracked open his beer, and ate at the sturdy pine table while he scrolled through his iPhone and updated social media. The radiator hummed and the pipes creaked in the background. The smell of sauce and meat drifted in the air. He embraced the quiet, settled in, and enjoyed the solitude. After dinner, he powered up his laptop and did a few hours of schoolwork, finally rubbing his tired eyes around nine o'clock.

To think he once had nothing to do but hang at the pub with his friends was now laughable. Most of the time, he fell asleep with his textbooks open on the table, drooling over the pages. Other than an occasional Saturday night out or hanging with his brother, his social life had dried up to an embarrassing level. He rarely saw his old friends, who were mainly into getting drunk at the bars every Friday and Saturday night, refusing to acknowledge that forty loomed dangerously close. Hell, the saddest part of all was he didn't even miss his old life.

Not even the women.

How had that happened? Not that he didn't have steady offers, but lately his sexual drive had been humming at a low level. Something seemed lacking in all of his encounters, and he couldn't seem to figure out the problem. He'd never been like his brother, craving some type of mythical connection with a woman that didn't exist. No, he believed hard in the three B's when it came to dating. They were part of his own personal Bible he'd created to keep things uncomplicated.

Beauty.

Body.

Boobs.

Marriage didn't interest him, and neither did getting tied up with all the daily routine and messiness of a long-term relationship. He'd seen firsthand how the feeling of love could turn bad and sweep everyone in its wake into a tsunami of casualties.

No, thanks. Keep it clean and everyone remained happy. He just needed to get his groove back.

He got up from the table and cleaned up. Maybe he'd spend a few minutes spacing out in front of the television. Yeah, he had to be at the job site at five a.m. for his construction job, but he needed to clear his mind from the array of numbers flashing in his head.

Dropping into the comfortable sectional, he channel surfed for a bit before he hit pay dirt. *The Fast and Furious* number—well, whatever. Nothing like some good car crashes and skimpily dressed women to soothe him. He put his feet on the coffee table and settled in.

* * * *

"How was school, honey?"

Her son dragged his fork across the chipped plate. "Fine."

Ella raised a brow. Luke slumped at the table, staring at his meatloaf with pure suffering. She didn't blame him. Lately, dinners were thrown together with little thought to gourmet taste and more to sustenance on a faster timetable. "Did you just utter the most boring, inane word on the planet that should be struck from Webster's Dictionary? The word I absolutely refuse to acknowledge in this house because I believe we have brains larger than an amoeba? Did you say the word—fine?"

He tried to look annoyed but his lip twitched. "Sorry. It was uneventful."

She grinned. "Much better." They smiled at each other and for a little while, life was just about perfect. Ella knew well about grabbing those moments in time that defined her daily routine. Her son was growing up. Every day, she felt as if he tugged another inch away from her toward the big bad world that was waiting to gobble him whole. Her gaze swept over his beloved face, with his charming pug nose, full lips, and graceful brows. His brown hair was thick and messy, with a terrible cowlick she'd never been able to tame with gel or scissors, but was such a part of who he was she hoped he'd never get rid of it. His round black glasses made him look like a young Harry Potter. Of course, he hated them and was already begging for contacts.

But his eyes were truly the window to his truth. A deep, rich chocolate brown, they reminded her so much of his father. Luke's were full of warmth, kindness, curiosity, and zeal.

His father's had been full of unfulfilled longing and too many secrets.

Ella tamped down a sigh. The last time she'd convinced Luke to sit on her lap for just a moment, his lanky legs had hung over her and hit the floor at an awkward angle. She'd spent her entire life engulfed in the magic of words and poetry, and in that moment, finally got what it felt like to grieve the passing of time. Just another one of those things you could read about or watch but didn't truly understand the flood of emotion until you experienced it. Kind of like childbirth.

"Besides uneventful, have you made any friends yet?" she asked.

His head dropped again. "Nope."

"No boys in the neighborhood? Maybe to ride bikes with or something?"

He snorted. "Let's just say there's been no welcoming committee. I'm fine, Mom. Don't worry about it."

And that's exactly why she worried. Luke was extremely independent, and usually had no problem making friends. His wicked sense of humor won over his toughest critics, but the past months had stolen his smile.

He needed more time, and she knew he'd make friends. Pushing wasn't going to help. Attending a new school simply sucked. She'd tried everything possible not to move, but the job offer at Verily College was a gift she couldn't pass up. She hated not being home after school for Luke, but for now she had no choice. Next semester she'd have a better schedule and more flexibility, but for now, she needed to prove herself and take the unwelcome time slots leftover from the other long-term professors.

Ten years old and already he'd experienced more pain than she ever intended. He'd lost his father, his home, and his friends. As his mother, she'd only wanted to protect him and make him happy. Make him feel safe.

Fail on all counts.

She pushed away her gloomy thoughts. "I thought we'd paint your room this weekend," she offered brightly. "You pick the color—anything you want. And we can hit Target for some decorations."

"Okay."

His despondent tone cut right through her heart. "Can you do me a favor, Luke? I need the honest truth."

He looked at her with a bit of wariness. "Sure."

"On a scale of one to ten, how bad is my meatloaf?"

The faint spark of humor lit his brown eyes. "One."

"Yeah, I thought so. How does a pizza sound?"

He tilted his head and considered. "Can we eat in front of the TV, too?"

Ella laughed. "Sure, why not?"

"No History channel?"

She gave a sigh of surrender. "Fine. You pick."

He gave a small whoop and fisted his hand in the air. "Nice. I want pepperoni on mine, please."

"You got it. Luke?"

"Yeah?"

"I love you."

His face shifted to that half uncomfortable, half pleased look she recognized so well. But he gave her the words. "Love you, too, Mom."

He bounded out of the kitchen, forgetting to clean up his plate, and Ella didn't remind him. She went to order the pizza.

Chapter Four

"When the doctors came they said she had died of heart disease—of the joy that kills."—Kate Chopin, The Story of An Hour

Two weeks later, Connor realized he was in trouble.

Another F stared back at him from his last paper. As Ella lectured to the class on the limitations of creative women in society today, Connor scrolled through his iPad for the picture he'd taken of the syllabus.

Yes, it was only a month into the semester, but he'd lost too much ground. He hadn't been able to pass one lousy quiz, flunked his paper, and now his short essay she'd handed back had tanked. Even with high grades moving forward and a decent curve, he'd be hovering around a precious C-, a bit too close for comfort.

No way was he letting poetry and angry female authors beat him.

Or Ella Blake.

He made a point to read the awful assignments, though he barely kept awake. This last essay called *Death of the Moth* should've been termed Death From Boredom. Woolf was another writer he struggled to understand, and Ella seemed to think she walked on fucking water. Who watched a moth die for what seemed like hours and decided to write about it? And why on earth would anyone assign a paper on such drivel? No wonder he'd flunked.

Men didn't do shit like that.

He'd been trying to get on her good side. He was unfailingly polite and charming before and after class. He complimented her and consistently offered to help out if she needed anything. She only gave him that icy stare that froze his balls and clipped out a "no." He was getting nowhere and now he needed to do something about his grade.

Anything.

He tried to listen to her ramblings on Edith Wharton and how the author used female roles in society to exploit and push readers' emotional limits. She strolled back and forth in a relaxed, steady pace as she spoke, occasionally nibbling on her lower lip in a thought, her face half hidden by the wide, thick frames of her glasses. Today, she wore her usual brown flat boots, a long wool skirt with no shape, and a green turtleneck sweater that reached all the way up to her jaw. Did she have some type of skin infection that kept her hidden beneath so much material? Were there actual breasts under there? Her fingers were long and tapered, but the short, squared-off, unpolished nails did nothing to accentuate them. This was a woman who didn't want a man looking. Or maybe she was just lazy and wasn't into men. Maybe she spent every night reading Wharton and Brontë and lived out fantasies in her head. Hadn't he read something in the news about the power of romantic novels to give women unrealistic expectations of life? Yeah. It had been in the *New York Times*, too. So it must be true.

"Mr. Dunkle?"

Ah, crap. Here we go again.

He showed no fear and smiled warmly. "Yes, Professor Blake?"

"I'm interested to hear your thoughts on the story, *Roman Fever.*"

"I liked it."

The class tittered. She never lost her smile. If she wasn't wearing the wrong color lipstick, he may have believed her lips were perfectly bow shaped and lush.

"I'm relieved. What did you think about the ending? Did you feel sympathy for Mrs. Slade when she discovered her friend was unfaithful? Or did it strike you as justice?"

He tried hard not to rub his forehead. A headache threatened. Out of all the damn stories she had to pick to discuss, this was the only one he didn't read. He'd fallen asleep at his computer and decided to skip the reading for today. Now he was in trouble.

He quickly gathered the threads of information the class had given and tried to make a rational theory. "It wasn't justice, but was it deserved? Probably. See, the problem is women are very different than men. They sink to a level of jealousy and cattiness I think is well described in this story."

Satisfaction unfurled. That was a solid answer. She couldn't torture him over his opinion.

Except the strangest expression came over her face.

Her gaze narrowed. Her lips tightened. A tightly contained energy swarmed around her like a nest of bees, humming madly before the attack. In that moment, he realized he had done something very wrong.

"I see. So you believe men don't sink to basic levels of human emotion like women?"

He swallowed. "Kind of. Men are more physical, but they see things simpler. Let's be real here. Two men would never meet in a cafe to talk endlessly for an hour before getting to the point. Women are exhausting. One man would punch the other one, they'd fight it out, and then go get a beer."

The class laughed. Some of the guys nodded in agreement and hooted their approval. Connor began to warm up to the subject. "And another thing. Society is always on the men about cheating, but if you read these pieces you keep assigning us, you'll see there was a lot of infidelity by women. They just like to intellectualize and rationalize the act to death to make it better for them to sleep at night."

Ella Blake never wavered. Pure ice dripped from her voice when she deigned to speak. "Interesting. It seems because Mr. Slade is the male, he is easily forgiven for his infidelity, though he has cheated also. Thank you for proving my point, Mr. Dunkle. Next time, please make sure you actually read the story and not use your classmates' effort to spin your own inane opinion. Class dismissed."

She marched back to her desk.

Connor's head felt as if it had gone a few rounds with the heavyweight champion. Was she kidding? How did she know he didn't read it? And who the hell was she to make fun of his opinion? If he *had* read the story, didn't he have the right to his own viewpoint?

Some of the guys came to clap him on the shoulder as they exited the classroom. He spent some time gathering his papers and cooling down his temper. He needed his grade fixed or he'd be in some serious trouble by the midterm. It was time to have a bit of a heart-to-heart and pour on the charm. Again.

He tried not to grind his teeth as he approached. She pretended not to see him, but Connor knew she sensed his presence and was deliberately provoking him. An odd anticipation steadily built. He'd misjudged her. She wasn't as dull as he'd originally thought. He rarely dealt with women who challenged him, but he figured it was the teacher/student thing that had him intrigued now.

"Professor Blake?"

She looked up and damned if she didn't give him an almost satisfied grin. "Yes?"

"I need to talk to you about my grade. The paper. I need some help."

"I agree, Mr. Dunkle. Perhaps a tutor?"

Instead of sitting down, she grabbed her purse and seemed to be rushing out. He made sure to step right in front of her, blocking her exit. He gritted his teeth. "I don't need a tutor. I need to know what you're looking for in my papers so I can start passing this class."

"Ah, if you check your syllabus, you'll see I'm looking for creativity, original thought, and specified examples and content backed up from the text."

"I'm trying! Let's be honest for a moment. You don't like my opinions so you're punishing me. You want me to advocate these inane texts by using a lot of fancy words and lingo just so I can agree that women were mentally and emotionally tortured underneath the societal restrictions where men ruled. How is that fair?"

She tilted her head, seemingly considering her words. "Now that's an argument. Too bad there's not more of that in your papers. I have to go. I'm late for a meeting."

She strode out of the classroom, big skirt swishing, hair perfectly contained in the single, tight space of her bun. Connor took off after her, refusing to be swept aside. Not this time. "I did put that in my paper but you gave me an F."

She never broke stride, weaving in and out of the hallways amidst groups of students. "No, you didn't. You said it was about a moth, written from the point of view of a woman frustrated with her life so she decided to spend her extra time watching an insect die. You insinuated she craved a man in her life and therefore, her lack of one made her unhappy. There was no depth. Did you even listen to my lecture in class about the meaning of the essay?"

"Yes." No. He kind of drifted off in a stupor when she began lecturing. He pushed aside the guilt. "You're not being clear enough."

"You're not trying hard enough, Mr. Dunkle. You treat my class like an annoyance and with little respect. I shall treat you the same."

"I need a C- in this class or I won't graduate. I'm doing the best I can. Are you seriously going to flunk me and keep me from my degree over a moth?"

She stopped and whirled around. Her saggy sweater caught air, flew up, then settled. Her index finger jabbed the air. "Have you ever wondered what death would feel like, Mr. Dunkle? Debated life versus death? Analyzed your life to see if it was empty or just or worthwhile?"

His head spun. She was like some mad woman, fierce and way too intense over some...words. Yet, that passion connected within him for a few seconds and hit home. "Yes. Don't we all wonder what we're doing here?" he muttered.

"Good. In the beginning of the essay, the moth was joyous, even trapped between the glass with a limited view of the world. Have you ever felt happy, even when you don't know why?"

"Yes."

"But the author pitied the moth at first. Pitied its existence. The moth is destined to die. What feeling did Woolf try to explain to the reader?"

He tried to shake off his annoyance at getting into a lesson in the middle of a hallway. "The moth doesn't want to die and neither does she."

"Wrong. Yes, no one wants to die but that's not the true point of the essay. There's one guarantee in this life: death. It's part of the contract terms we get. We don't even know how much time we're going to get when we sign this contract. We're here trying to make our mark, then we're gone. Don't you ever consider what the point is?"

His gut lurched. Her slow pecking at his beliefs bothered him. Why think about all this shit when there was no real answer? Why not keep things easy? Look for happiness in the moment? Like the moth...

"Sure."

"Enough with the one word answers. *Just as life had been strange a few minutes before, so death was not as strange.*' What do you think Woolf was feeling when that last paragraph was written? She watched the moth die in front of her, watched its struggle, watched its failure to win the ultimate battle. What do you think about that, Mr. Dunkle?"

"What do you want me to think?"

She shook her head. "We're done here."

Frustration simmered and seeped out. "The moth fought death up to the last moment. Its struggle was strange and almost beautiful to the author because we all face the same obstacles, yet no matter how bad life sucks, we still have the ability to fight to our last dying breath. Kind of like Dylan said about raging against the dying light."

Surprise flickered across her face. Slowly, she nodded. "Yes. That's what I'm looking for in your papers. You insult both of us by not giving more." Then she continued down the hallway.

Son-of-a-bitch. No, he wasn't in one of those lame movies where the teacher suddenly got the student to see the light and then he transformed his failing grade into an A. It didn't work like that. Connor caught up with her, matching her pace, and heard her deep sigh.

"Do you need something else, Mr. Dunkle?"

"How about an extra credit project? I can't base my graduation on me understanding the next few assignments."

Her snort was quite feminine and intriguing. She pushed open the double glass doors and headed upstairs. "Why should I give you such an opportunity? If you work hard enough, you should be able to pass my class."

"I can't take any chances. Please. This way, I'll know I have some cushion for my grade if I keep struggling."

Annoyance radiated around her. She reached the top of the steps, and turned to say something, but her boot caught on a piece of metal grating and she fell forward.

Connor hurriedly blocked her fall, catching her in his arms and pulling her to the side. Her body was soft and warm, and for one moment, he felt her breasts push against his chest. The clean scent of cucumber and soap drifted up to his nostrils. Low maintenance and simple, like the woman. He took a deeper breath, enjoying the natural fragrance and the way her hands closed around his shoulders for balance.

"You okay?"

Her dark eyes widened. Behind the thick lenses of her glasses, her gaze locked and held his, squeezing him as tight as her nails suddenly digging into his flesh. A bolt of heat struck his dick, and suddenly, he was hard as a rock.

WTH?

"Sorry!" She struggled and he righted her, stepping back. Her skin flushed and she scrambled toward the second level doors. "I'll think about an appropriate project for extra credit."

"Thanks."

She didn't answer, just disappeared behind the glass and got swallowed up by a swarm of students.

Shaking off the whole strange encounter, Connor headed to the library. He'd won this skirmish. With extra credit, he usually had the whole semester to turn it in and his grade would get a nice boost. As for the sudden attraction? It was proof he'd been way too long without a woman. He wasn't attracted in the least to Ella Blake. If he was smart, he'd take this Saturday night, go out with a pretty woman, and slake both of their needs.

He kept the thought firmly in his mind and refused to think of his not hot professor.

Chapter Five

"Better to be without logic than without feeling."—Charlotte Brontë

A few hours later, Ella was still replaying their encounter.

She muttered under her breath and hurried through the parking lot, ducking her head against the brisk wind tearing through the trees. She'd had students who were egotistical and arrogant. But Connor Dunkle was a whole new breed. How dare he challenge her in class? His ridiculous views on women were archaic. Lord help his wife or girlfriend. She would've taught him a few hard-learned lessons about respect. Then he dared to ask for extra credit?

The worst part was her traitorous body. When she fell into his arms, her stomach got all floaty, and her blood ran hotter in her veins. She was attracted to an idiot. Why wasn't she surprised? Her track record sucked.

Rain dripped down the back of her neck and she shivered. Spring felt a lifetime away. Of course, she'd forgotten her damn umbrella again. She had four in her trunk and never seemed to use any of them.

The well-lit parking lot cut through the dark and fog, leading to her white Honda Civic. She hit the button, slid into the seat, and turned the key.

Nothing.

Dread trickled through her. Oh, no. Please work. Please work. Please...

Keeping up her mantra, she tried the car again. And again.

It was dead.

Ella glanced at her watch. She was already running late and hated leaving Luke alone for too long. Her brain calculated through the possibilities. Triple A? No, she'd decided it was an easy expense to cut. She couldn't look under the hood because she had no idea what she'd be looking for. Frustration coiled and she pounded her fist on the steering wheel. The word hovered on her lips until she finally spit it out with passion.

"Fuck!"

God, she loved that word. Saying it was her secret vice. Even the guttural, nasty sound of it on her tongue eased some of her tension.

A hard rap on the window caused her to shriek. A huge, muscled figure towered over her car. Peering out in the dark, she lowered her window a few inches.

"You need some help?"

Ella almost closed her eyes in defeat. Connor Dunkle. Of course, he'd show up trying to be her knight in shining armor. He'd probably ask her for a few extra points on the next quiz as payment.

She refused to think of other, more interesting, forms of payment.

"My car won't start. I'll call a tow company. Thanks anyway."

A frown creased his brows. "Pop the hood. Let me take a quick look." She pressed her lips together, considering. "Professor Blake? I'm getting wet out here."

She let out an irritated breath at her hesitation. "Sorry." She was glad the dark hid her hot cheeks. Releasing the latch, he disappeared behind the hood while the rain gained fury and flung drops like a toddler in the throes of a tantrum. Finally, he returned, his thick hair wetly plastered to his head.

"It's the battery. I have jumper cables in my truck. Hang tight."

"Wait! I have an umbrella."

His smile was lopsided and full of wry humor. "Don't need it. I work construction, I'm used to bad weather."

"But—"

He'd already disappeared into the dark. A pair of headlights swung toward her as he angled his truck a few inches away from her car. She watched while he set up the cables, seemingly unaffected by the weather, and motioned for her to start the car.

The engine caught.

Relief cut through her. He gave her a thumbs-up and walked back to the window. "Keep it running a bit before you start to drive. Where are you headed?"

"Home."

Again, that grin appeared. Her heart did a slow flip-flop at the flash of strong, white teeth. Why did he have to be so damn attractive? So...viral? "I know. How long is the drive?"

"About half an hour."

"I'll follow you."

She shook her head. "That's unnecessary. I'll be fine. Thanks so much for your help."

"I'm following you," he said. "If you want to call your husband or boyfriend and let him know, that's cool. I'm not a killer or anything."

A garbled laugh escaped her lips. "I'm not worried about that. I've already felt helpless enough watching you start my car in the rain. I can get home by myself."

"It's still raining and you're keeping me here arguing. What if the battery dies again? I'll worry until I know you're safe at home. Wait for me."

His command struck her mute. She wasn't used to men wanting to do stuff for her. She'd been on her own long enough to make her own rules and was never questioned. Instead of feeling lonely and bitching about it, Ella had embraced the independence and began to like running her life. This was the first time she'd been overruled.

He was worried about her. It was kind of nice in an old-fashioned type of way.

Connor unhooked the cables and got back into his car. She hit her lights, cranked the heat to maximum, and slowly pulled out of the lot.

The commute home was slow. Cautious drivers took their time and traffic built up, but the headlights behind her stayed steady, giving her a strange type of comfort. She called Luke on her Bluetooth and told him about the delay, and he agreed to start on his homework. Finally, she pulled onto her block by her building and cut the engine. Her escort parked right behind her. Grabbing her purse, she darted out of the car to quickly thank him, but he was already climbing out. The rain had finally slowed to a lazy drizzle.

"Thanks again for the help. I'm really sorry I took you so far from home."

He stared at her building and shook his head. "You didn't. In fact,

I'm already here."

"Huh?"

His gaze narrowed and those stinging blue eyes caught and held hers. The scent of rain and the subtle spice of his cologne rose to her nostrils. His next words seemed to be a premonition of everything in the future that was about to change.

"I'm your neighbor."

"Wh-what? I haven't seen you around here. I don't even recognize your truck."

"My apartment comes with a driveway so I park over there." He jerked his head toward the back of the lot. "I think I saw your son. About nine years old? Glasses?"

Shock delayed her response. Out of all the people in the world, Connor Dunkle was her neighbor. The air shimmered around her, and the rain turned to a misty, glowing aura. She smothered the emotions running through her, screaming out she never believed in coincidence and there was a bigger reason for such a discovery. "Yes, Luke. He's ten. I-I had no idea. He didn't mention running in to anyone."

"I interrupted an encounter with some boys. He got pissed at me. Do you want me to introduce myself to your husband? I don't want him thinking I'm some stalker."

"No need. I'm divorced. What boys?"

"A group from the neighborhood. I'll keep an eye out. They get in to some trouble, but Luke seems to be able to handle himself."

She needed to talk to her son. Tell him to keep his distance from troublemakers. God, this is when she missed having his father around. "I better go. Thanks again."

"Ella?"

She stilled. It was the first time he used her first name, and it sounded oddly intimate spilling from his lips. "Yes?"

"If you need anything, just let me know."

She muttered another thank you and hurried away. She didn't want to think of Connor in any other way than a pain-in-the-butt student. Having him right next door and conversing with her son shifted the balance. She really knew nothing about him on a personal basis. Until she did, Ella better warn her son to keep his distance.

Damp, tired, and cranky, she pushed her way inside.

* * * *

Ella Blake was his neighbor.

Connor chewed over this fact for a while before deciding it could be a good thing. Hell, if he helped her out a bit, maybe she'd soften and give him a better grade. Being a single mother was tough. After his mother took off and his father checked out, taking care of Nate sapped all his effort and energy. It made more sense why she didn't take more care with her appearance. Men were probably the last thing on her mind. Still, if she ever wanted to find another relationship, she'd need some extra help.

He let himself into his apartment and wondered what it would be like to be with someone more than a few nights. Nate seemed happy, but then again, he'd always seemed to want a woman on a permanent basis. Connor was content experiencing the whole buffet, and not once had he wanted more. Was there something lacking in him? And if so, maybe it was for the best. If he was built like his mother, he may end up running out on responsibilities, and he'd rather die than hurt someone like that.

Of course, lately he'd give a monk competition. It had been so long since he'd had sex, his condoms probably had cobwebs on them.

Shaking his head at his own personal humor, he reheated some leftover pizza, opened up his laptop, and concentrated on work. He'd only been at it about an hour when his phone rang. He glanced at the ID and hesitated. Then picked it up.

"Hey, Jerry. What's up?"

The slight slur of words told him his best friend was on his way to feeling really good. "Connor, my man! Where the hell you been? Fancy college boy now and can't come out and have a few beers?"

A flare of guilt hit. When was the last time he'd seen him? Weeks. They'd been really tight working construction for a number of years and had each other's backs. Until Connor had begun wanting more. More than getting drunk every weekend. More than seducing some new woman into bed. More than blaming management for all their trouble on sites and pretending they were better than anyone else because they got their hands dirty.

The fun had begun to turn bitter. Especially when he'd made the decision to get his degree and apply for a management position.

Connor forced a laugh. "I've missed you, dude. Been dying to get out and share a pint, but I'm slammed with schoolwork."

"Didn't think you'd try and become one of them. What happened to you, man? Those books get to your brain and make you think you're something you're not?"

The words cut deep, but he kept his tone easy. "Nah, I just got a few more months and this will all be behind me. Keep my chair warm, okay?"

"Fuck the classes, man. Come and have a drink with me. There's a pretty young blonde serving me that's dying to meet you."

Half of him wanted to go. It would be so easy because it was the routine he'd followed for the majority of his life. He'd get a good buzz, bed the blonde, and be happy for a few hours.

The problem was the next morning when reality hit. When the blonde left and he had a sick stomach, lighter pockets, and the faint tang of failure in his gut. Not this time. Not anymore.

"I'll catch you next time, dude."

Jerry cursed. Then hung up.

Connor clicked off and rubbed his forehead. He felt like a traitor. Jerry and him went way back, and his friend was old school. He believed in working hard on the site and partying harder when he was done. Unfortunately, times were changing and management wanted more from their crew as things became more technological and architecturally modern. They wanted team members to grow with them, not just show up to put in time.

Connor wanted one thing: secure the lead foreman job for Bilkins Construction. He'd been lucky enough to be included on the subcontractor team for the huge project with Tappan Zee Construction, which was building the new bridge over the Hudson River, but he needed more. It was the only reason he'd spent the last two years breaking his ass to stuff four years of school into two and still make an impression at the firm. Bilkins only hired college graduates for upper management. Connor was determined to transform himself into a businessman who could straddle both worlds—the one on a working site and the one behind a fancy desk.

Finally, his efforts were working. The higher-ups noticed him and respected his work ethic and his leadership role with the crew. He'd changed his life radically to become the man he'd always wanted to be but never thought he'd deserve.

Was he betraying his friend by wanting more out of his life? An emptiness clawed up from deep within him he'd never experienced before. He wasn't sure how to feed it, so he concentrated on the only thing he could control right now.

Graduate. Get a promotion. Make more of a difference. Then maybe, the hunger would go away.

He sat at his desk for a while, then got back to work.

Chapter Six

"I don't know if I should care for a man who made life easy; I should want someone who made it interesting."—*Edith Wharton*

"Mom? I'm bored."

Ella slipped off her glasses and rubbed her tired eyes. Glancing at the clock, she noted it was already past five p.m., and darkness had slipped over to blanket her most precious Saturday. Not that she'd done anything great. Food shopping, cleaning, a few rounds of the Wii with her son, and then grading papers.

Now, Luke stood in front of her desk with puppy dog eyes and a young boy's leashed excess energy. Winter sucked. Sports were nonexistent, the holidays were over, and he was already bored with his new video games and stuff from Christmas. She kept waiting for him to invite some friends over, but he hadn't seemed to make any connections yet. A few times, she spotted a small bunch of boys out front talking to Luke while he waited for the bus. She didn't want to ruin anything by being his pushy, overbearing mother, so Ella kept quiet and hoped he'd make his own way.

She gave him a smile and ticked down the list of available items to entertain a ten-year-old. "Wanna see what's playing at the movies?"

"Nah. They just have lame stuff for kids."

"You are a kid," she teased. Her fingers itched to ruffle his cowlick but he was becoming a bit more standoffish with her treating him like a baby. "You too old now for Disney?"

He rolled his eyes. "Can we go to GameStop?"

She raised a brow. He gave a defeated sigh.

"Wanna bake cookies? I have some leftover holiday ingredients. You can try to bake the biggest cookie in the world."

He seemed to consider the option, though it was obvious he wondered if it was too babyish. She upped the ante. "Then we can walk to the Chinese restaurant and get soup and eggrolls. We'll eat backward. Dessert first, then dinner."

"You still have the sprinkles and green M&M's?"

"I do. But you better be prepared. I'm going to win the cookie challenge. We each get a tray and no peeking until we're done. Deal?"

"Deal!"

She cleaned up her work and headed to the kitchen. Though their apartment wasn't huge with a big yard and fancy furniture, Ella had made it home. Using her knack for brightening up rooms with accessories and a fresh coat of paint, the two bedrooms were cozy and peaceful. The kitchen was big enough so she purchased a mobile island and topped it with mesh baskets full of bright fruit and dried herbs. Pictures crowded the walls with her favorite sayings from poets, and she'd upgraded the low utility light to a pretty Tuscan chandelier that brought pop to the room. The farm table and benches were set by the big window to get the most light. Hand towels beautifully stitched hung by the stove and dishwasher.

She tuned to one of her playlists on her iPhone and cranked the volume. Queen ground out *Another One Bites the Dust* and she slipped out two cookie sheets while Luke pulled all the ingredients out of the cupboards. They belted out the lyrics in perfect tune and began kneading dough into cool shapes in an attempt to dazzle the other.

Contentment flowed through her veins as she relaxed into her typical Saturday night. She pushed back her hair with sticky fingers and rainbow sprinkles flew up in the air, getting stuck in her sweater.

The lights went out.

Everything ground to a stop except the music, which kept blaring loud. She reached over and turned off the music, switching quickly to the flashlight app.

"Mom?"

"Don't panic, sweetheart. Probably just a brownout or something. Let me get some extra flashlights just in case."

"This is kind of creepy."

She felt around in the dark for her famous junk drawer that contained so many weird parts she probably could've built a nuclear bomb. "It's a nighttime adventure. Remember when I used to take you on those walks when you were little?"

"The moon had to be full, you always said. Even though I worried about werewolves."

"I told you they don't exist."

"But you're afraid of vampires."

"Well, I think they *do* exist. That's why I keep tons of garlic around at all times. I read *Dracula* three times, you know."

That got her son to laugh, and Ella finally found another flashlight. She was just going to brave going into the basement to check the circuit breaker when the doorbell rang.

Her heart pounded. She didn't know anyone to drop by on them, and she'd heard of strange things happening during brownouts. Swallowing, she eased over to the window and peeked through.

Connor Dunkle stood on her doorstep.

With a rush of relief, she flung open the door and held back a gasp.

My God, he looked good.

Struck mute for a moment, she gave in to impulse and hungrily took him in. Dressed in a button down navy blue shirt that clung to his broad chest, a casual jacket, and dark-washed jeans, he simmered with delicious masculine testosterone. Usually a hint of stubble clung to his square jaw, but tonight he was clean-shaven and smelled of spicy cloves. His thick dirty blond hair fell in waves over his forehead, brushing his ears, and those sea blue eyes framed with thick lashes struck her mute for a few seconds. He towered over her in a mass of rock-hard muscle, giving her the impression of both strength and protectiveness.

He was a walking, talking specimen of everything a woman dreams of in a man. Both Hemsworth brothers mixed with Daniel Craig and a sprinkle of old-fashioned Redford. Her poor body roared into overdrive and she felt a damp rush of moisture between her thighs.

God, she was acting like a sex-starved teen. So. Embarrassing.

Finally, he spoke. Even his damn voice was gravel and satin mixed together in a symphony to the ears. "I saw your lights went out. Looks like some of the other houses on the block are affected. You okay?"

He was checking on her? To be nice or to get her to agree to extra credit? "Yes, we're fine. Thank you."

"Did you flip the breaker? Sometimes these apartments get overloaded and you need to reset it. That's what I had to do with mine."

"I haven't gone down to the basement yet."

"I'll help you out."

"Oh, you don't have to."

His gaze sharpened on her face, and his jaw clenched. Fascinated, she studied his features, noticing the air of irritation that briefly shone. "I want to, Ella. I won't stay. I just don't like the idea of you and Luke alone in the dark."

She flushed and stumbled back. "I didn't mean to be rude. I'm just used to doing things for myself. I'm sorry, come in."

He walked inside and she realized it was a mistake.

In her home, he owned the small space, filling the air with a masculine presence she wanted to sink in and savor. It had been so long since she had a man close. Even though he was only here to check her electricity. Oh, my God, she was so pathetic. He glanced around in the dark and took out his own phone, turning on the flashlight app.

Luke came out of the kitchen, highlighted in the sudden glare of light. "Mom? What's going on?"

"It's Connor Dunkle from next door," he said. "How's it going, Luke?"

Her son's voice hardened. "Fine."

"Good. I'm going to check the basement and see if I can get those lights on. Is that okay?"

Connor didn't move, as if waiting for permission from her son as the man in the house. Luke seemed to consider his words, standing up straighter in the beam of light. "Yeah, that's okay." He paused. "Can I help?"

"Absolutely. I could use a hand. Basement here?" He motioned down the hall toward the door on the left. Ella nodded. "Same as mine. We'll yell if we need you."

They disappeared downstairs, and she tried to re-gather her composure. Why was she nervous? So silly. He was just being a friendly neighbor and helping out a single mom. Clatters rang in the air. Probably moving all the storage stuff to get to the panel. She really needed to organize better down there. Ella waited, keeping her light trained down the hall, and suddenly the electricity flickered back on.

She heard Luke's whoop and smiled. She forgot the simple things that gave children pride. He really didn't have the advantage of tinkering with tools or cars or talking sports, though she tried to keep her knowledge up to date and be both mom and dad.

They both reappeared with pleased expressions. Connor was talking to her son. "Next time, check the breaker first. Now you know which one since we tagged it."

"Got it," Luke said seriously.

"Hey, you guys were making cookies? Looks like fun."

She glanced at the mess in the kitchen and wrapped her arms across her chest. "We know how to rock a Saturday night. Thanks for helping out."

"No problem. Oh, man, I love M&M's!" His face lit up like a kid, and Ella laughed. "Can I have one?"

"You can't eat just one," Luke said. "Here." He gave him a handful. "I like the greens."

"Blue is better."

"They taste the same," Ella pointed out.

They both stared at her in disbelief. Connor rolled his eyes. "Women."

Luke grinned. "Mom, I need to check my DS. I had it charging and I don't want to lose my stuff."

"Sure, go ahead."

He bounded up the stairs, leaving them alone in a messy kitchen. Ella looked at Connor's perfect appearance and tried not to wince at the thought of her image. Dough in her hair, mismatched socks on her feet, and yoga pants. "Umm, thanks again," she offered.

"No problem. Been a long time since someone baked me cookies. Sounds like a perfect night."

She looked at him with suspicion. Was he making fun of her? "They're easy now. Precut dough, one sheet, and an oven. Not too mysterious anymore."

Ella caught a flash of pain reflected in those gorgeous eyes before it was quickly masked. "Moms bake them the best. If I was Luke, I'd be pretty happy right now. You're a good mom."

Pleasure ran through her but she fought it off. "How do you know?"

He shrugged. "Just do."

"Thanks. You look nice. Going somewhere fun?"

"Got a date."

"Oh, that's nice." Why did she keep saying the word nice? And why were her palms suddenly sweating and her heart beating fast? She was in her own house, for goodness sakes. "I'm sure you'll have a good time."

"Yeah. Rather be here, though. Bake some cookies, hang out and watch a movie."

She laughed then. "If you had my life, that would be your routine every weekend. Somehow, I think yours is more glamorous."

That assessing gaze swung back to her, taking in her disheveled appearance. She fought a blush, refusing to apologize for being real in her own place. "Have you dated since you split up with Luke's father?"

He seemed surprised by his direct question. She was even more surprised when she answered. "No. It's hard. I wanted to make sure Luke was ready, and then I just got too busy. I wouldn't leave him alone at night anyway."

"I'd watch him for you."

She jerked back. Blinked. "You'd watch Luke for me while I went on a date?"

"Sure. We're neighbors. He seems like an easy kid. I know it must be hard, so I'd do you a favor."

It all came clear then. Her lips pursed in disapproval. "Oh, I get it. A favor for a favor, huh? I give you an extra credit assignment or a grade boost and you watch my son?"

She expected guilt or denial, but pure disgust flicked out at her in waves. "That's a crappy thing to say. Why are you so damn prickly all the time? I'm just trying to be nice."

"But you want me to give you an extra credit assignment?" she pushed.

He threw up his hands. "Hell, yes! I want to pass your class. But I'm not doing nice stuff for you just to get a better grade." He raked his fingers through his hair and she watched the strands settle right back in perfect disarray. "I may have thought that before, okay? But I swear it has nothing to do with your class. It's separate. We're neighbors, I respect you, and the offer stands."

Warmth flooded through her. He was honest. He seemed nice to her son. And even if he was screwing up with her class, he was open to do the work necessary to pass and graduate.

She had the perfect project for him.

Ella nodded. "Fair enough. I'll send you the details of the project in your e-mail on Monday."

"Really?" He stared at her with suspicion. "You're not setting me up or something, are you?"

She smiled. "No. To keep it fair, I'll offer it up to anyone else in the class who wants to bring up their grade."

He studied her face for a while. "It's going to be bad, isn't it?"

"Let's just say you'll learn a lot."

"God help me," he muttered. "But I won't look a gift horse in the mouth."

She winced. "If you want to boost your grade, stop using clichés in speech and written language. It's unnecessary."

"Yes, ma'am."

She shook her head at his mocking tone, walked to the door, and opened it. He yelled good-bye to Luke and she stepped out with him to study the block. "Looks like everyone is back on. Thanks again for—"

"Connor!"

She turned her head. A gorgeous redhead strolled down the street, her three-inch Michael Kors boots clicking on the pavement. She was wearing one of those trendy hats that made Ella look ridiculous, along with clinging leather pants, a leather jacket, and some sparkly T-shirt. Connor raised his hand in the air.

"Hi, darlin'! Be right there."

The model nodded agreeably, crossed her ankles with easy grace, and waited like a trained dog.

Connor smiled. "Sorry. That's my date."

Ella blinked. Together, they'd look more dazzling than any Ken and Barbie couple on the planet. "You didn't pick her up?"

"No. She wanted to pick me up."

Of course she did. Ella looked back and forth between them. Irritation scraped her nerve endings. "And you let her? Don't you think that's rude?"

He shrugged. "No, women like to be independent."

"She's waiting for you outside, in the cold, like a trained seal? You think that's independent?"

"Sure. I let her pick the restaurant, too."

"Is she also going to pay the bill?" Ella asked sarcastically.

Connor looked affronted. "I always pay. Look, women like to call the shots. Give them attention and some compliments and they thrive. It's simple. Not rocket science."

"Do you always date beautiful women?" she asked slowly.

"Sure. We both get what we need, and things are kept...simple."

Coldness washed over her, erasing the slight glow from seconds before. Connor Dunkle was an ass. He treated women like playthings, concentrating on the surface, rarely taking time to dive underneath. The quick pang of hurt surprised her, but she buried it and got real. Yes, he was a sexually attractive man that sent her hormones on a roller coaster ride, but he was immature, and there had never been a question of anything more between them then professor/student or neighbor to neighbor.

"Understood." She separated herself by backing into her warm, safe house, alone with her son. "Have fun."

After she shut the door, Ella couldn't help but peeking out the window. The leggy female walked toward him, pressing a kiss to his lips, laughing at something he said. They both climbed into a low-slung red sports car like the fabulous couple they were and tore off into the night for their glamorous date.

Depression threatened but she fought it back. She absolutely refused to let herself feel bad that she wasn't out on the town, pretending to be someone she wasn't with a man who couldn't care less.

She raised her voice to call her son and concentrated on cookies.

Chapter Seven

"A divorce is like an amputation: you survive it, but there's less of you."—
Margaret Atwood

Connor hated Valentine's Day.

It was the only holiday structured toward the demise of men.

He muttered under his breath, pulling on his winter jacket. In the middle of the darkest month of the year, society created it for commercial reasons only. They got to jack up the price of flowers, chocolate, and dinner bills in the name of love. A complete breeding ground of discontent for women not getting what they wanted, while the poor bastards they were with scratched their head in confusion.

Another great reason not to have a relationship.

Or maybe he was just in a bad mood because he still hadn't gotten laid.

Why hadn't he slept with Tracey? The date had been perfect. Dinner, cocktails, flirting. Her offer to join him wasn't wrapped up in heavy analysis or layers of meaning. Yet, as he opened his mouth to answer, "Hell, yes!" he told her it wasn't a good night but he'd call.

His date had ended with him and his hand. Not the image he'd pictured.

Something was wrong with him. Tracey was gorgeous, and had proved to be a good lover in the past. He had a little black book that bulged with numbers and he still wasn't using it to call anyone. Maybe his overworked mental state was affecting his drive for sex? Usually, he looked at a pair of perfect boobs and was ready to go. Lately, he got lukewarm.

Except when he was around Ella. A woman he was completely not attracted to, yet his body responded to like a switch had been flicked. A woman who barely allowed an inch of naked skin to show. That was plain scary.

He remembered what she looked like when she opened the door. A total mess. Yet, instead of focusing on the cookies in her hair or her misshapen sweater, he'd noticed her lack of glasses and hypnotic eyes. He'd noticed the scent of sugar and candy, and her pretty bare feet with pink toenails. He'd noticed the tumble of luscious dark waves that spilled over her shoulders. He'd noticed the clinging Lycra emphasizing her lean calves.

He was nuts. Around the bend. Loco. All the clichés Ella hated.

He grabbed his gloves and tried not to think of her. Since that night, she'd sent over the extra credit project, and Connor had wondered if it was worth it. It was as bad as he imagined.

Woolf. Brontë. Austen. Not separate, but all together in one big mishmash of readings and a big fat paper due at the end of the semester. She was punishing him, and he knew it. He dipped a toe in the water—another damn cliché—and began perusing *A Room of One's Own* by Woolf and was stopped cold.

Yep, more feminist fiction. More whining and "poor me, we're under men's control and we hate it" philosophy. But damned if he wasn't going to kick ass on this assignment and graduate. Even if it killed him.

Which it might. From boredom.

The air was brutally cold, warning of the storm about to roll in. Time to get the plow ready. He had a solid list of clients to make some extra money in the winter, but he'd be extra busy the next two months trying to handle the workload. He checked his watch. He was later than normal, especially if he wanted to stop for coffee on the way to Verily College. He headed out the door and heard a shout. Looking toward the driveway, he watched a bunch of boys scramble away from his truck and race down the street, whooping in loud, excited shouts of victory.

Connor ran to his truck, a curse blistering past his lips. Little shits had slashed one of his tires. The right passenger was totally flat, a jagged slice ripped through the rubber.

Hell, no. They weren't getting away with this.

He took off after them. His long legs made up time from their shorter strides. He caught a flash of red up ahead, then something flew through the air and dropped on the ground. Darting around corners, they picked up the pace, and age finally triumphed. By the time Connor got a few blocks down, they'd disappeared, their voices fading in the sharp, cold air.

Sons of bitches.

He knew it was the gang that had picked on Luke. He'd need to get some security cameras installed or set up a watch. Probably was retaliation for the DS incident. Catching his breath, he walked back, mad at himself for not pushing faster, and noticed a black object on the pavement.

He picked it up and turned it over in his gloved hands.

Glasses. Black rimmed glasses like Harry Potter.

Ah, crap. Was Ella's son now involved with their gang? He seemed like a good kid, but maybe he'd gone the other route. Join the bullies rather than be picked on. He didn't blame him. Sometimes, it felt like the easy way out, but no way was he getting away with this. Ella needed to know.

Connor headed back and inspected the damage on the tire. He had a spare, but these suckers were expensive. Pushing away his irritation, he walked next door and rang the bell.

Her face reflected the same irritation he felt. He figured she'd be friendlier after his visit, but in a way, she'd grown even colder. Her dark hair was twisted tightly back in a severe braid. Today she wore baggy tweed trousers, black waterproof boots that looked squishy soft, and a black turtleneck. The only color was her lips, which thankfully were bare from her usual orange garish color. "Hi. Is something wrong? I'm running late."

Her politeness rubbed his nerves. Even as his professor and next-door neighbor, she treated him with icy politeness. Hadn't he offered to babysit and help out? Hadn't he proved he wasn't a jerk? "I think your son vandalized my car."

She jerked back. Her mouth made a little O before her brow snapped into a frown. "That's impossible. Luke would never do anything like that. What happened?"

"My tire was slashed by the gang of boys who likes to hang out around here. I think I saw Luke running away with them."

She blew out a breath. "Trust me, you're mistaken. He still doesn't have many friends, and he's a good boy. He would never hurt someone or their property."

He lifted the evidence. "Are these his glasses?"

Ella blinked, then slowly reached out to take them. "Oh, my God. Where did you find these?"

"Scene of the crime. They were running from me and one kid dropped this. Does he wear a red jacket?"

"Yes. But-but this is impossible. Luke doesn't do things like this, I swear to you. They slashed your tire?"

He nodded. Regret flowed through him. He knew kids did bad things sometimes, it was part of life, but he had a gut feeling Luke could go down a wrong turn. His parents were divorced and he'd moved to a new school. Ella had said his dad wasn't around a lot. That was a lot of shit to deal with. "He's probably acting out. Who knows what happened. Do you want me to talk to him?"

She shook her head, dark eyes filled with grief. His heart squeezed in sympathy. "I don't know. Maybe I should handle it? I'm so sorry about this. I can call the school right now and find out what's going on."

"No, don't. Let him finish out the day and feel guilty. It's the best punishment for a kid like Luke. If it's okay, I'd like to offer him a deal to work off the tire."

"I'll pay for the damage, Connor. I feel terrible—this has never happened before."

He shifted his feet. How involved should he get with this? He didn't want to pretend he knew what she should do, but he knew Luke's behavior needed a strong hand. "I'm not worried about the tire, Ella. I've been through this stuff before. I'm not trying to tell you how to be a mom, but I had issues like this raising my brother. I'd like to tell Luke he needs to pay off the tire by working for me. It shouldn't be your responsibility, and if you pay for him, he'll figure he won."

She tilted her head in interest. "What type of work?"

"I do snow plowing with my truck in the local area. Have a list of clients. I usually shovel out their pathways manually. Luke could do that for me."

Ella nodded slowly. "Sounds fair."

"I also have some projects I'm working on in between work and school. Building my brother a shed up in Verily when the snow stops. He can help and I can teach him some stuff."

Those brown eyes narrowed as she studied him. Once again, the golden swirls around her irises intrigued him, as if trying to tell him there was something deeper about Ella Blake if he only one took the time to look.

Not that he had the time or interest.

"You have a very busy schedule," she finally said.

"I told you that in class when you agreed to give me extra time for my paper."

Surprisingly, her lips twitched in a smile. "You did. But I never agreed to more time."

"Right. That was me being an ass."

This time, she laughed. "You're learning." Curiosity lit her gaze. "You had to raise your younger brother? Did something happen to your parents?"

He always avoided talking about his past. Other than his brother, he wasn't one to share emotions or delve into painful history. But he found himself telling her anyway. "My mom took off when Nate was about ten. Dad pretty much fell apart in a drunken stupor, so there was no one around. We didn't have any other family. I just took over."

Ella stared at him for a long while. "He was Luke's age? How old were you?"

He shrugged. "Fourteen. I was able to handle it." He couldn't help the proud grin that escaped. "Nate's a genius. He worked for NASA and now he's employed by a private company working on space travel."

"He got through college with a scholarship?"

"Half of it."

"Did loans pay for the other half?"

"Nah, I didn't want him in debt. I worked a few jobs and saved so he had most of it paid."

"You worked a few jobs when you were a teenager? And paid for your brother's college on your own?"

He shifted uncomfortably. "Yeah. Honestly, it wasn't a big deal. I was working steady by sixteen. Dad had the mortgage and main bills paid at least, even though we rarely saw him. I'd never been great in school anyway, and Nate is gifted. He got the brains in the family. It made sense for him to go."

"I see," she said softly. Why was she looking at him funny? As if she was seeing him for the first time? "But you're in college now."

"I'm going for management. The company I work for won't promote anyone who doesn't have a degree."

"You decided on Verily. That's a hard school to get in to."

"They offered me credits for life experience and my current work, so I was able to chop some time off. I got lucky, too. Scored high enough on the college entry exams."

"Did you go the full four years?"

He wondered at the odd inquisition but kept answering. "Nah, I stuffed four years into two."

"Other than my class, what's your GPA?"

"3.9."

"But your brother is the one with the brains, huh?"

Her gaze stripped away the lies and got to the truth. No wonder she was a good teacher and an awesome mom. No one could hide under a stare like that, whether he wanted to or not. He'd never talked about himself this much before. Hell, the whole evening with Tracey they'd flirted, talked pop culture, and discussed her acting career. Nothing about him. Yet, here he was, spilling his guts while he stood in his neighbor's doorway.

Suddenly uneasy by everything she seemed to see, he cleared his throat, trying to get back his footing. Another cliché. Why was he noticing every simplified thought when it had never bothered him before?

He gave her a smile and fell back into his usual female mode. "Hope I didn't ruin your Valentine's Day. I know it's an important day to women."

She shuddered. "I despise Valentine's Day. I think it was created to completely torture the male species and force women to feel bad about themselves if they're not in a picture-perfect, sugar-coated, commercially driven relationship."

He lifted his brow. Who would've thought they'd actually agree on one thing? The standard words fell from his lips without thought. "I'm sure there's a line of men who are waiting to take you out tonight. You're pretty as a picture. You just have to get out there. My offer to babysit still stands."

He waited for her to blush or smile, but instead she glared. "That's the stupidest line I've ever heard in my life. We both know there's no line. I'm not pretty. And you're using those ridiculous clichés again that I hate. Why do you have to cheapen a genuine conversation with such drivel?"

His mouth fell open. "I was only trying to give you a compliment. Make you feel better about Valentine's Day."

"No, you weren't. You were trying to make yourself feel better by believing inane lines spoken to women actually make them feel good. You were being lazy because God forbid, you take the time to actually find out who someone really is. Your so-called compliments insult both of us. Don't you ever get real, Connor Dunkle?"

Shock poured through his system. How had this happened? Her son vandalized his car and suddenly she was insulting *him*? He dealt with reality every single damn day. "Hey, I'm the one being attacked for being nice. Ever consider that your adversarial ways are blocking you from getting a date?"

"I'm not looking for a pretty face to date. I'm looking for someone who's not afraid to get messy and see the pearl buried under the dirty, closed-mouthed oyster. Have you ever done something for a woman without waiting for a pat on the back? Or given a compliment on anything other than her appearance?"

"I respect a woman's brain. It's not my fault your entire gender is so obsessed with their appearance, body, and age. Women crave approval and reassurances that they're beautiful. Don't get mad at me just because I give you what you really want."

She shook her head in disgust. "Bull. You don't bother to dig deeper because you choose not to. You don't know how to relate to creative women who aren't afraid to get ugly and tell the truth. It's easier to see the surface image, isn't it? Like your date," she added with a slightly bitter tone.

Temper hit him. How dare she question his intentions? She knew nothing about him. With a low growl, he leaned forward and challenged her back. "Oh, yeah? You think you haven't judged me by my appearance? By my job or my apartment? I work construction, Ella. I have blistered, raw hands, crazy shifts, and don't own a suit. I'm thirty-eight years old without a college degree. I don't live in a fancy house and I'm not a fancy guy. Who's not being real by saying you never judged me by my appearance?"

The breath gushed out of her lungs and she took a step back. Silence descended as the angry words hung in the air between them. He shook his head in disgust. There was no reason to get upset by the truth. Women saw him as an attractive guy to have sex with but not marry. They ogled his body, not his brains. Most women he dated had no interest in a real conversation unless it was a segue to bed. Nate was the marrying kind. Stable, financially secure, wicked smart.

Not Connor.

"Forget it. This whole thing is ridiculous. I gotta go. I'll check in with you later about Luke. Happy Valentine's Day."

He stomped off without another word and refused to look back. But her words lingered in his mind for a long, long time.

* * * *

Valentine's Day was officially her nemesis.

From the moment Connor knocked on her door, things had drifted into a steep decline. Her son had committed vandalism. A crime. It was completely opposite who he was as a person and how she raised him. Her stomach curled with nausea until she wanted to just drive to the school and confront him. But she agreed having some time to deal with his guilt—hoping he had some—would be a good lesson. After all, she'd seen it a zillion times portrayed in *The Brady Bunch*.

School was a fog of battling concentration between the ridiculous hormones of college students on a national holiday for love. No one seemed interested in her lessons, preferring to talk about plans for the evening or showing off presents received from companions. The break room and cafeteria were cluttered with ridiculous stuffed animals that had no purpose, too much candy, and balloons formed in the shape of hearts. Her coworkers were just as guilty as the students. She'd caught Bernard, the history professor, trudging down the hall with two-dozen roses in his grip and a silly grin on his lips.

Awful. Just...awful.

Late morning, she looked frantically for her glasses and ended up finding them when she sat down and heard a solid crunch. When she pulled them from under her lap, the broken frame dangled limp between her fingers.

The word vibrated beneath her chest, dying to escape, but still Ella fought it back. Cursing was not a solution to the problem. The day had to end sometime, and then it would be over for a whole year.

By the time she got in her car to drive home, the roads were slippery from the snow beginning to fall. She tried to distract herself with music, but Frank Sinatra crooned on too many stations. When she punched the buttons, sappy love songs filled the speakers.

She clicked it off and drove through the snow in silence, squinting. Dammit. Her spare set of glasses was at home.

An hour later than usual, hands trembling from the slick roads and tension of not being able to properly see, Ella pulled to the curb and cut the engine. She mentally rehearsed the speech she'd been practicing for Luke. Grabbing her briefcase and purse, she tiredly pushed through the door.

And blinked.

"What's going on?"

Connor and Luke sat on the couch. Two mugs lay on the coffee table. They looked like they had been in deep conversation, and when they heard her voice, both jumped to their feet, looking almost guilty. "Sorry, we didn't hear you come in," Connor said. "How are the roads?"

"Terrible. What are you doing here?" she asked.

Connor looked down at Luke and something passed between them. Connor gave a slight nod, and her son stepped forward.

"Mom, I'm sorry. I screwed up bad."

Her heart pounded. At least he was going to confess. His beautiful dark eyes looked sad behind his glasses, and his shoulders slumped in defeat. Swallowing back the need to go comfort him, Ella dropped her bags and sat down on the leather recliner facing him. "Go ahead."

He took a shaky breath. "I slashed Connor's tire. With a group of boys from the neighborhood. I didn't want to, but I—I got mad. I got tired of being on the outside and not having any friends, and they dared me and called me a pussy, so I did it."

Emotion choked her throat. God, it was so hard to be a kid these days. But life was going to get harder, and more difficult choices had to be made. If she didn't do her job and teach him how important every decision was, she wouldn't be giving him the right tools. She kept her face impassive, letting him see her disappointment. "Connor came to me this morning and told me," she said. "He found your glasses. Are you admitting this because you got caught?"

He shook his head. "No. I felt sick all morning. I didn't know he saw me. When I got home from school, I went next door and told him what happened."

Connor spoke up. "He's telling the truth. He apologized and offered to make it right. So we came back here to wait for you, so he could tell you himself." Connor placed a hand on Luke's shoulder and squeezed in reassurance. "I told him my day was shot because I had to get a new tire, but I respected him being man enough to own up to it."

Stupid tears burned her eyes. To see the flash of satisfaction in her son's eyes for being called a man broke her heart. Yes, he'd made a big mistake, but he made it right. It was the most she could ask for, and she ached to hug him tight and not let go for a long time.

Instead, she cleared her throat and nodded. "I agree with Connor. I'm proud you took it upon yourself to tell the truth. Can you tell me who these boys are? What do you think we should do about them?"

"They're not in my school, Mom. They're older. I don't see them every day. At first, they gave me a hard time, but then they said if I proved myself, I could be part of their group."

"Do you know their names so I can contact their parents?"

"I've seen them before, Ella," Connor interrupted. "They drift in and out of the neighborhood, looking for trouble, but I haven't been able to track down where they actually live yet."

"They said Connor needed a lesson because he's always interfering with them."

"Are they dangerous?" she asked. What if they began stalking Luke? Or tried to physically assault him? "Should I call the police?"

"They've never done anything before," Connor said. "I think this was more about Luke than me. But I've ordered some security cameras for outside my house. I picked up some for you, too, with a monitor. I'll install them tomorrow."

"You don't have too, I'll—"

"I want to." His tone warned her not to argue. "I talked to Luke about working off the tire and wanted to see if it was acceptable to you. We decided he'd help me out with shoveling on my jobs. When the weather clears, I'll also need a hand building a shed for my brother. He's agreed to both."

"I think that sounds fair," she said softly. "When do you want to start?"

"Tonight," Luke piped up. "I did my homework. Connor said he needs to go out for a few hours and I told him I could start right away. Is that okay, Mom?"

She studied her son's face, surprised he didn't look gloomy or despondent about his fate. He actually seemed like he was looking forward to it. Was he lonely? Or did he just crave some company other than hers?

"Of course. I can make dinner for you both, if you'd like. Then you can head out."

Connor grinned. "Would love to jump on that, but I need an hour to work on my paper. I have this teacher I'm having a hard time impressing. I'll pick you up at six, Luke."

"Thanks."

Connor headed to the door, then swung back to motion to her son. "Don't forget to give your mom her present."

"Present?"

"Oh, right. Wait here!" He rushed out of the room.

Connor grinned. "Was your day as bad as mine? Hey, where are your glasses?"

She reached up and touched her naked nose. "Sat on them. My spare is upstairs."

"Damn, you did have a bad day."

She laughed. "Yeah, it was a doozy. I'm surprised you don't have a hot date tonight, though."

"Nah, they jack up the price for everything and there's no one special that's really worth it."

Ella rolled her eyes. "You're such a romantic."

"Yeah, what's your excuse? Why do you hate V day so much?"

The memory tore through her, but the pain was just a slight throb, a reminder that she hadn't been enough. "My husband left two years ago on Valentine's Day," she finally said. "He said I didn't inspire him anymore."

Silence fell.

Why had she told him that? Such a deeply personal fact of her life? Embarrassment made her cheeks hot but she forced a laugh. "He probably just wanted to save himself some money. He'd been buying me all sorts of trinkets because of guilt from his affair. Now, I realized he did me a favor."

He still didn't speak. Thank God, Luke came running back in and thrust a huge bouquet into her hands. Shock filled her. She gazed at the beautiful flowers, blood red with perfectly formed petals eliciting just a touch of scent. Her son had never bought her anything before. Her voice trembled. "Luke, these are beautiful! Thank you so much."

"Happy Valentine's Day, Mom," he said.

And then he walked into her arms without pause.

She hugged her son and the flowers close to her chest and lifted her gaze.

Connor watched them, ocean-blue eyes filled with an intense longing that stripped away the delicate barriers and dove deep into her soul. She knew in that instant, he'd been the one to get her the flowers. He'd been the one to suggest it to her son.

Her breath caught, and a swirling mass of hot energy sizzled between them, choking her with a want she'd never experienced before. Where had this come from? And why did it feel like it was growing each time she saw Connor Dunkle?

Fighting her rioting emotions, she closed her eyes to try and get back control.

When she opened them again, he was already gone.

Chapter Eight

"The Eskimos had fifty-two names for snow because it was important to them: there ought to be as many for love."—Margaret Atwood

"You were right about the flowers," Luke said.

Connor headed to his last stop of the night, maneuvering carefully on the roads even though his tires were stellar with their grip. He'd never had a kid in his truck before so he drove extra slow.

"I told you, women like to be appreciated. Especially Moms. Especially on Valentine's Day, even though it's not my favorite holiday."

"Mine either. Christmas is so much better."

He laughed. "Yeah, Christmas is pretty epic. We have one house left and then you've completed your parole time for the day. You did well."

Pride etched the boy's features. Funny, Connor figured the night would be torturous trying to entertain a ten-year-old, but Luke was good company. He owned a wicked sense of humor and worked hard without grumbling. Shoveling pathways and steps worked muscles most boys didn't have anymore because they mostly worked out by playing video games. Bet his grades were off the charts, too. He reminded him so much of Nate. "Is this your regular job?" Luke asked.

"No, I just do this as extra side work. I'm in construction. Right now, I'm working on the team that's building the Tappan Zee Bridge."

"Seriously? That's awesome. Do you go up on the crane?"

"Sometimes. Most of the time it's hard, repetitive type work in the extreme hot or cold. Sometimes it's real boring, but I like working with my hands and watching a structure rise from nothing."

"How come you're in my mom's class if you already have a job?"

He eased around the upcoming turn and cranked the heat a notch higher. "I want to get into management, and they require a degree. Don't make my mistake. Go to college after high school. It's harder when you're old like me and have to start over."

Luke seemed to mull over his words. "Mom says people do things when the time is right. Maybe you just weren't meant to go to college when you were younger."

Luke's simple acceptance of fate soothed him. Ella's words wrapped around him via her son's lips. He'd never forget her face when she told him about her ex leaving. A mixture of sadness and acceptance had radiated from her and made him want to pull her into his arms and comfort her. He couldn't imagine how hard it was to hear her husband tell her she wasn't wanted. The asshole had just walked out on a beautiful family and didn't seem to care about Luke. Her heart and trust was shattered, yet she seemed more whole than any other woman he'd known. She was truthful, and real and smart. Not to mention strong. She'd kept it all together and was raising a good kid.

The more he found out about her, the more he liked her. Underneath that drab exterior beat the heart of a very mighty woman. She'd looked different without her glasses. More touchable. More...vulnerable. If she only took more care with her appearance, she could probably meet a nice man who would be good for her and Luke. A conservative type, maybe. A man who was stable and employed, and appreciated all of her qualities.

Nate's girlfriend, Kennedy, owned a matchmaking agency called Kinnections. She'd teased him mercilessly about not setting him up until he went through social training to be more sensitive to women. Connor had just laughed it off. One thing he didn't need help with was finding dates. Women had always come easy to him, though he'd only fallen in love once. The memory still stung but it had been his own stupidity thinking he was good enough for more than great sex. He'd been thinking long-term future. She'd been thinking short-term orgasms. Eventually, she'd cheated on him and moved onward, not pausing to look back and see how she trampled his damn heart.

His fault.

But Ella could use some help and Kennedy had a magic touch when it came to makeovers. She'd completely transformed Nate and promptly fell in love with him. Could she do the same magic for Ella?

Connor pulled up to the house and parked. "Okay, dude, you're up. I'll plow the driveway and you work on the steps. Last call."

"Got it."

Luke slid out, grabbed his shovel from the back, and trudged through the growing mounds of snow. They both worked quickly and thoroughly and finally headed back home.

"Luke?"

"Yeah?"

"Have you decided what you're going to do when the Little Rascals show up?"

His statement had the desired effect. Luke grinned. "I like that. The Little Rascals."

"Thought you would."

Luke gave a long sigh. "I don't know. I just want them to leave me alone. I was stupid. I'm just sick of not having someone to hang with at school."

"Are there any guys you'd like to hang with?"

He nodded. "Yeah, there are two that seem tight and they're cool. But they kind of keep to themselves."

"I hear you. You're not going to want to hear this, but I'm going to say it anyway. They're not going to approach you. You need to man up and ask if you can hang with them. Either at lunch or recess."

The boy gnawed at his thumbnail. "I don't know. I'll look like an idiot if they say no."

"If they say no, it's really not a big deal. It's not like you're asking them on a date, dude. You just want to have a few conversations."

He laughed again. "Maybe. I'll see."

"What are they into?"

"Pokémon cards. Basketball, too, but we can't play outside until it gets nicer."

"You got any Pokémon cards?"

Luke snorted. "Of course. Got a whole binder full."

"That's your in. When you approach them, talk Pokémon. Usually you just need something to break the ice a bit." Connor mentally winced. Another cliché. Damn Ella and her crazy tyrannical English.

Luke tilted his head, obviously thinking over his suggestion. "Good idea."

"The weather's not going to be pretty the next couple of days. I'll talk to your mom, but are you up for helping me out?"

"Yeah, no problem. I'm alone every day until Mom comes home anyway. I do my homework and stuff but sometimes it gets boring."

"Same as me. My shifts start early. Other than Tuesdays and Thursdays, when I have your mom's class, I'm home in the afternoon. If you ever want to do homework together, just come over. And if you've ever read Virginia Woolf, come by with your notes."

Luke laughed. "Okay."

They drove back in comfortable silence, and Connor dropped him back off at the house. He watched him disappear inside and he parked the truck, his spirits light. Luke was just like his mother. After a while spent in his presence, it became easier to find ways to like him.

He settled in for the rest of the night with a smile on his face.

Chapter Nine

"Love is like the wild rose-briar; Friendship like the holly-tree. The holly is dark when the rose-briar blooms, but which will bloom most constantly?"—Emily Brontë

The next couple of weeks, Connor settled in to a comfortable rhythm.

Luke accompanied him when he needed to plow, and they got into a habit of stopping at the diner afterward for cheeseburgers. On Monday and Wednesdays, he showed up with his homework and hung out until Ella got home.

Connor was used to being solitary, so it surprised him how easily he fell into a new routine and began to look forward to spending time with Luke. Through him, Ella had softened and often invited him over to the house for dinner. As the grueling winter hurled its fury in various ice and snowstorms, they huddled inside for warm food, hot cocoa, and sometimes the occasional board game.

His paper began to take shape at a slow, grueling pace. Sometimes, he'd bitch about the convoluted style of feminine whining from her assignments, but now she just laughed and challenged him by offering up various facts and shared stories about their lives that were so vivid, he found himself reluctantly intrigued.

Connor wasn't sure when it happened, but he knew somehow, some way, they'd become friends.

He refused to analyze the reason or try to dig deeper. He was too afraid if their odd relationship was examined too closely, it would disintegrate under a strong wind and disappear forever.

He usually worked on Saturdays, but he found himself with an afternoon free and no motivation to take on an odd job or do homework. The snow had melted just enough to clear the roadways, and the upcoming March week promised sun and a good thaw. On impulse, he walked next door and rang the bell.

Luke answered, his face lighting up when he saw him. "Hi, Connor. Come on in."

He stepped inside and Ella came around the corner. Her hair was twisted up in a messy knot, and she held a broom in one hand, with a dirty rag in the other. She gave him an evil smile and crooked her finger at him.

"Ah, he's stepped into our lair, Luke. You know what that means, right?"

"It's a fate worse than the plank. Worse than the guillotine."

Connor glanced between them, grinning at their silliness. "You guys are seriously scaring me."

"Any brave soul who ventures forth in the Blake household has to clean!" Ella declared.

"I'm outta here."

Luke laughed and blocked the door. Ella held the mop out like the Wicked Witch about to cast a spell on him. "Too late, Dunkle. You get the bathroom."

"Forget it. I came to see if you guys wanted to go snow tubing, but since cleaning seems more fun, I'll go check with someone else."

"Snow tubing!" Luke jumped up and down. "Mom! Can we go?"

Ella wrinkled her nose. "But we didn't finish cleaning."

"Mom! Please, oh, please. I swear I'll finish later when we get home. Some of the guys at school were talking about it, oh, please."

Connor crossed his arms in front of his chest. "That's some mighty fine begging, Mom. But I don't want to break up you and Mr. Clean."

Ella made a face. "Cute. What do you need? Snow pants and boots?"

"Yep, that's it. We rent the tubes there. Up for it?"

"Mom?"

The whine was perfectly pitched and coincided with puppy dog eyes. Ella let out a breath. "How can I say no when I'm outvoted? Let's go."

Luke gave a whoop and raced up the stairs. "I'm gonna change!"

Ella looked down at her mop in mourning. "I guess no one ever died from dust bunnies, right?"

"If so, I would have suffered a horrible death years ago."

She punched his shoulder in a playful motion and touched her hair. "Ugh. Give me a few minutes to freshen up."

"Sure."

She came down in record-breaking speed, gliding down the stairs in black snow pants, a baggy sweatshirt, and snow boots. He was used to women who spent hours creating a palette on their face and a runway look for their wardrobe. Ella was comfortable in her own skin, didn't care what she wore, and owned both with a confidence that had originally puzzled him, but now he admired. Still, he much preferred her pale pink natural lips than the orange she sported. He wondered if he could steal it from her purse and help her lose it permanently.

They drove to the snow tubing park and hit sheer chaos. Kids swarmed the hills with giant black tubes, and a contraption that worked like a ski lift pulled them to the top of the hill. Screams and laughter cut through the air. The mountains shimmered in the distance, jagged white rock framing blinding blue sky. The air rushed deep and clean in his lungs as they trudged to the cabin to register and get tubes and got in line to wait.

"Mom, you're not going with us?"

She shook her head. Cheeks flushed from the cold, she laughed and slid her glasses back up her nose. "I'll pass on this one, guys. You two causing a spectacle is enough for me."

"A spectacle, huh?" he said. "Never pegged you for a snob, Ms. Blake, but I may need to rearrange my original opinion. When was the last time you did something completely undignified?"

She rolled her eyes at his deliberate language. Luke chuckled.

"Yeah, Mom, you should go. It'd be a riot to hear you screaming as you slide down the hill."

Her brows snapped down in a frown. "Are you both baiting me? I would not scream."

"Care to make a bet on that?" Connor drawled.

Her lips pursed and irritation simmered around her. He'd learned she was kind of a sore loser. When he won at Monopoly, she accused him of using the green real estate to drive them out of business. When he beat her at Bananagrams, a game similar to Scrabble, she claimed he'd used abbreviations and slang. When he found poop in the actual dictionary and reigned champion, she got all snarky and muttered under her breath the rest of the night. It was kind of cute.

"What bet?"

He pondered her question. "You go down the hill once without screaming and I'll take you both out to dinner. Your choice."

Luke whistled. "That's a good bet, Mom. You've been craving Italian for a while now but said that place was too expensive."

Connor raised a brow. "Care to take the bet?"

She glared at both of them, then stomped her feet. "This is the stupidest thing ever. I'm going to get wet and be miserable, but the lasagna will be worth it. Also the literal egg on your face."

Connor smiled slowly. "Nice cliché."

Her mouth fell open in shock.

"Save our place. I'll grab you a tube," he told her. Laughing the whole way, he got another one and when he rejoined them, they were almost to the top. The attendants were brisk and efficient, setting them up on the lift and showing them how to hold the tube as they were pulled along. When they reached the summit, they were each set up in their own row, with Luke all the way to the left and Ella on the right. Connor was in the middle.

They waited their turn and then the attendant gave them the thumbs-up signal.

Everyone pushed off at once.

Connor slid down the hill with decent speed, especially since his arms and legs were dangling over the tube, slowing him down. He spun in a full circle, the wind whipping at his face, stealing his breath, and laughter poured out of him as he reconnected with childhood memories of him and his brother spending a snowy day together.

Luke got up first. "That was awesome! I'm getting back in line right away."

"Okay, go ahead."

Luke rushed back to the line and Connor looked for Ella. Where was she? His heart started to pound furiously, and finally he spotted a tag of black to the far right of the hill. How had she gotten over there?

He bounded down the slight hill and found her spread out on the snowy ground, eyes closed, deadly still.

"Ella!"

He bent over her, cupping her cheeks, looking for any injuries. Her eyes suddenly snapped open, causing him to jerk back.

"Gotcha! I didn't scream once, Dunkle. You owe me a lasagna."

He stared at her in disbelief. "I thought you were hurt!"

She rose up and smiled slow. "I know. Now who let out an undignified scream? What'd you think, I got hurt from a little snow tube? I'm tougher than that. Where's Luke?"

He shook his head and stood up, reaching out his hand. "He's back in line. You know, people have gotten head injuries from this sport. Next time, have a little consideration."

She looked a bit chagrined. "Sorry. Geez, I didn't know you'd get so worried." She reached out and took his hand. In one perfect motion, Connor pretended to pull her up, then dropped her back so she tumbled into the snow.

His grin was evil. "Oops. My bad."

She glared at him, shaking snow out of her hair. "You're gonna pay for that."

"Bring it."

They stared each other down and then moved. In a flash, she went for him, but he pinned her down and they wrestled in the snow bank, rolling over and over until her giggles reached his ears and he finally stopped.

"Okay, okay, get off me. You win."

Her knot had loosened and thick inky black waves covered her face. Slowly, he pushed them back from her cheeks and stared down at her, smiling. "You're a real pain in the ass, Blake."

She stuck out her tongue.

When he'd first met her, she struck him as the intense type. A real dry academic. Not much fun. He preferred the impulsive, easy, flirty type of women who didn't take themselves so seriously. But over the weeks, he'd discovered Ella's sense of fun was childish and pure at heart, like Luke's. Simple things gave her joy. Their gazes locked, and suddenly, everything changed.

The air charged. Simmered.

Sexual energy blasted to life. Crackled.

Raw arousal struck him hard. Squeezed.

She sucked in a breath. Hypnotized, he took in the lush pink mouth that had been rubbed free of lipstick. The gold-rimmed irises within eyes so dark and deep, a man could sink forever and never want to be pulled out. He leaned over. Her breath struck him with soft, breathy wisps.

"Ella?" he whispered.

Her lips parted. "Connor?"

They paused on the barrier, reluctant to take the tumble, frozen in place by the question asked of each other.

Connor made the only decision available because if he didn't kiss her in this moment, he'd spend the rest of his nights grieving the lost opportunity of a lifetime.

So he kissed her.

He swallowed her moan and tasted pure sweetness, an intoxicating swirl of purity and lust in one delicious twist. Her lips opened under his without hesitation, not only allowing entry but demanding. Her hands closed around his shoulders and she held on with a brutal force that rocketed his desire. Laid out on the snow, tucked away from the crowds, Connor kissed her like he'd never kissed another woman, and when he finally pulled away, he knew nothing would ever be the same again.

They stared at each other in pure shock.

"You guys okay?"

The deep voice cut through the fog. Connor jumped up, turning around to see one of the park attendants. He hoped his voice would work when he tried to use it. "Yeah, sorry. Had a bit of a wipeout. Thanks."

"No problem. Want me to take your tube?"

Ella stumbled to her feet, looking dazed. "Umm, yes, I don't need it anymore. Thanks."

"Sure." He took the tube and trudged away.

Ella averted her gaze. "I better go check on Luke."

"Ella?"

She shuddered. Wrapped her arms around her chest. "Yeah?"

He searched for the right words but didn't know what he really wanted to say. "I'm sorry."

She stiffened. "Don't be ridiculous. We were just caught up in a moment. It was silly. Let's forget it, okay?"

He tried to study her face but she turned and headed up the hill. As he followed, Connor wondered if he'd be able to forget it.

* * * *

She'd kissed Connor Dunkle.

Ella nodded and smiled as Luke chattered nonstop through dinner. He'd met two boys from school during snow tubing and spent some time with them in the arcade. Watching her son bloom from sullen to joyful filled her with such relief her muscles seemed to actually sag. The weeks spent with Connor had been good for him. He never complained about shoveling, and got into the habit of doing his homework next door with Connor. They'd gotten close, and a bond had developed between man and boy she'd never seen before.

Of course, it was dangerous.

Especially after the kiss.

Ella sipped her wine and picked at her salad. Luke was her main priority, and she didn't want him to be confused with the relationship between her and Connor. Somehow, they'd become good friends. He was also still technically her student. She wasn't about to screw anything up just because she had a physical weakness and was tempted by rock-hard muscles and stinging blue eyes. She'd need to forget the way his thighs had pinned her in the snow, parting her legs just enough so she could feel his erection through his jeans. She refused to think about the drugging, addictive taste of him on her lips, or the way his tongue had slid inside her mouth and taken charge with delicious, drugging thrusts.

No way. They had a good thing going, and she knew how Connor worked. Women fell into his path like they'd been hypnotized, helpless against the mix of gorgeous looks, physical stature, and melting charm. She wasn't the type of woman he dated or looked for in a mate. She had small boobs and dressed like a sparrow rather than a peacock. She had no idea how to flirt or play games. She had no desire to have a one-night affair and wreck their friendship. Pretending that kiss was anything but an impulse, quickly forgotten, would be disastrous.

The encounter proved one thing to her. She needed someone in her life. It was time. The image of the business card from Kinnections flashed in her mind, and Ella knew what she was going to do.

"I'm going to the bathroom," Luke announced.

"Okay, honey."

Her son left them alone. An awkward silence descended.

"Ella?"

She dragged in a breath and forced herself to look up. "Yeah?"

His blue eyes filled with worry. "Did I screw up? With us?"

She wondered what she'd do if he boldly stated he wanted her. Woman to man. Naked. When he kissed her, she'd experienced such an intense bolt of hunger, her body had wrested control of her mind and let her fly free. Maybe this was a sign it was time for her to begin searching for what she needed. His kiss proved she had her own needs. It had been two years since she had a date or sexual experience. Hadn't she sacrificed enough yet? She loved her son, but didn't she deserve to find love or companionship, too? Wasn't it her turn?

Ella forced a smile and shook her head. "No. We're friends, right? We're not going to let a kiss ruin that for all of us."

Relief flickered over his face. "Good. Wouldn't want to lose the best neighbor I ever had. Or Luke, of course. He's an incredible kid."

"Yeah. I'm kind of crazy about him."

"He seems to be happy. Making some friends."

They stared at one another for a bit. Again, the connection hummed between them. Ella cleared her throat. "So I made a decision. Remember when you offered to babysit for me?"

"Yeah?"

"I may need to take you up on that. I found a card for a matchmaking agency called Kinnections. I'm calling them to start the process."

"Did you say Kinnections?" he asked in disbelief.

"Yeah, why? Have you heard of them? They're located in Verily."

He shook his head and grinned. "My brother's girlfriend is an owner."

They were interrupted when the waitress came back and placed their dinners on the table. She was young, with pretty blonde hair, a short black skirt, and a gaze that focused solely on Connor. Ella bit back her irritation while she fluttered around him and completely ignored her. He shot the girl his standard, charming smile, and she practically sighed with pleasure.

"Thanks, darlin'. I appreciate you working so hard."

The girl boldly stared at him, cat green eyes hungrily roving over his body. "Don't mind working for a man who appreciates it."

"Well, I do appreciate it. Your pretty face brightened up my day."

Ella blanched at the awful line, but the girl smiled with pride. "Well, you can brighten my day anytime."

What? Oh, she was so going to lose it.

Ella cleared her throat. "Yes, thanks so much for doing your *job*. We're good." The waitress shot her a glare, then slunk away. Ella pointed her fork at him. "What's wrong with you? I don't care if you flirt with every female in a skirt, but why do you have to sound like you have zero intelligence? I mean, *darlin*? You're not even Southern!"

He frowned. "I was just trying to lift her spirits. Waitressing is hard work."

She ground her teeth in frustration. "Then don't thank her for having a pretty little face! Thank her for working hard and anticipating our needs as customers. Ugh, it's like you dragged womankind back a few decades. How do you get away with this stuff?"

He gave a suffering sigh. "Now you sound like Nate and Kennedy. I never had complaints before, okay? Women seem to like it."

"Well, they shouldn't. And if they do, you're dating the wrong type of women," she muttered.

"Can we go back to our original subject? I can call Kennedy and tell her you'll be calling. She may even be able to give you a discount. I'm excited for you. They screen all their clients and match you with a guy who's right for you. It's thorough and safe."

She picked up her fork and dug into her lasagna. Did he have to sound so damn excited about her suddenly dating? "Sounds good."

He began eating his ravioli. "They do a consultation and a makeover, too. It's all included in the price."

A flash of pain cut through her. She'd never be a woman to inspire a man to rip off her clothes and tumble her on the ground. But she'd be damned if she'd settle for the dregs of his pity for the poor, single mom. Did he want her to get a makeover that bad? If he was so turned off by her appearance, had he kissed her out of obligation? To make her feel better about herself? Shame burned.

She tried to keep her voice light and teasing though she squirmed inside. "Didn't know you were so excited about hooking me up, Dunkle? Trying to keep me distracted for a bigger curve on your upcoming assignment?"

He grinned. "Nah, I know how that works now. No more pissing off my professor. I just think you deserve to be happy, Ella. You're, well, you're—" he stopped off, shaking his head. He rarely stumbled over words or compliments toward females, so she studied him with interest.

"I'm what?"

"You're an incredible woman," he said softly. "You deserve...everything."

She sucked in her breath. Raw emotion flooded her system, but she had no time to answer. Luke came racing back, shoveling spaghetti and meatballs in his mouth in between trading bad knock-knock jokes with Connor.

Ella told herself to forget his intimate words and the way he made her feel. He was right. It was time to move on.

It was time to join Kinnections.

Chapter Ten

"A woman, especially, if she have the misfortune of knowing anything, should conceal it as well as she can." —Jane Austen

Spring rolled in like a lamb, leaving the lion's roar far behind. The days turned sunny, and as the snow melted into oblivion, flowers and trees peeked their heads out, deciding it was safe to finally come out and play.

He'd cleared the weekend to work on his brother's shed and swung by to pick up Luke and Ella. He smiled as they trotted out and climbed in the truck. "I'm surprised you wanted to come with us," he said to Ella. He took in her loose jeans, rain boots, and hooded sweatshirt. Though it was warmer, they'd be working outside so he'd told them to dress warm.

"I wanted to meet your brother," she offered, buckling her seat belt. "Also Kennedy said to come and keep her company while you do manly things."

Luke grunted from the back. "That's right, Mom. Maybe you can make us lunch while we build the shed."

She rolled her eyes at his poking. "Wise guy. Turn on the HGTV channel and half of the contractors are women. Is this how I raised you to think of females? Or have you been hanging out with Connor too much?"

They laughed. Connor threw up his hands. "Hey, if you want to take over, I'll be happy to prepare a meal in the warm house."

"Point taken. I'll stay inside."

"Good choice."

He drove out to Verily, radio blaring loud, windows cranked halfway down. He was so used to being with them it was almost like his own family. He'd grown close to both of them, and other than the odd electricity that crackled between them, Connor settled into a comfortable routine of companionship.

He never thought about the kiss. Well, hardly ever. Sometimes, the memory snuck up in the night, taunting him with the brief flash of her body underneath his, the sweet taste of her lingering on his lips. He'd never been affected by a simple kiss, but Connor figured it was the typical male game of wanting what he couldn't have. He wasn't about to risk losing Ella and Luke over a physical reaction that would pass after one tumble. He'd done it again and again. The next morning, Connor rarely felt anything but the need to move on. He'd never hurt Ella like that by playing games. She'd become too precious.

He refused to delve further into his strong feelings for the two people next to him, choosing to do what he did best. Just enjoy the day, moment to moment.

He drove past the familiar white sign welcoming them to Verily, and headed down Main Street. Nate had been begging him to move here, but the rents were a bit pricier, and his current place was a shorter commute to work. Still, he loved the small Hudson River town. Quaint and artistic, shops lined the streets, lights strung over the large oak trees, and popular cafes set up tables and chairs for guests. They passed the used bookstore, the Barking Dog bakery, and Kinnections, the matchmaking agency owned by Kennedy and her two friends, Kate and Arilyn. The dog park was packed on a sunny afternoon, and he grinned at the crowds of people with leashes gathering for social time.

He reached Nate's house in a few minutes and pulled into the driveway. They'd moved out of their old apartment and bought a small cottage house with a spacious yard, quirky slanting red roof, and a wraparound porch. His brother came out with Kennedy at his side.

"Hey," Nate said in his standard greeting. He grinned and leaned in for a half hug. "Good to see you, man."

"You, too. Looking good, little brother. Growing your hair?"

Kennedy laughed and enveloped him in a bear hug. "No, he's refusing to see Bennie for a trim until he finishes this round of testing on his current prototype. He's living in the lab. Thank goodness you're here to force him to breathe some fresh air."

Connor hugged her back. His future sister-in-law—well, one day he hoped—was a vibrant, commanding woman who stole Nate's heart at first glance. Her looks were dazzling, from her caramel-colored hair, curvy body clad in designer clothes, and whiskey gold eyes. But she was so much more than knee-buckling good looks to Connor. She was a friend, supporter, and made his brother happy. She challenged them both on any bullshit, pushed them to their limits, and loved them unconditionally.

She was family.

"Gonna help us build this shed, Ken?" he teased. "Bet you have cute little pink work boots and a matching hammer."

She tossed her hair in dismissal. "As if. Now introduce me to this charming young man who's going to break a million hearts."

Luke flushed from the attention but stared at Kennedy like she was a movie star. "I'm Luke."

"Nice to meet you, Luke." She shook his hand. Nate followed. "I've heard great things about you. Thank you for helping us build a shed. Nate has so much equipment, we can't jam it in the house any longer. Hi, Ella! I'm so happy you came to keep me company."

They hugged. He didn't get much information, but it seemed she'd already had her consultation, counseling appointment, and was moving forward with securing a date via Kinnections. He trusted Kennedy would keep her safe and set her up with the right man.

His gut squeezed at the sudden thought she wouldn't really belong to him anymore. But of course, that was stupid. They were only friends, neighbors, and teacher/student. Ella had never been his in the first place.

He shook off the strange emotions and ruffled Luke's hair. "Okay, dude. Let's get to work."

Ella and Kennedy wished them luck and disappeared into the house.

The supplies had already been delivered and were spread out in the backyard. He'd marked out the ground on his last visit, and the plans had been carefully plotted and confirmed with the proper zoning authorities. He called them over and explained the drawings to Luke, going over safety rules and the jobs he'd be responsible for. The boy listened and took it all seriously, his face etched with excitement for his first official build.

"Luke, the first thing we do when we're getting ready will set the tone for the day. Know what it is?"

He shook his head. "What?"

Connor shot his brother a knowing look. "Take control of the music before your partner does. If you don't you'll end up getting tortured by Mozart or bad country songs. Power up my phone, young man."

Luke laughed and turned away.

Nate gave him the middle finger.

Yeah. It was going to be a great day.

* * * *

Ella sat at the high counter in the breakfast nook, her gaze sweeping over the house. "I love your place," she said, taking in the gorgeously designed pieces that made the rooms pop. From the canary yellow rug to the massive red vase filled with exotic dried blooms, her senses were filled with delight. Lush green plants scattered about, the furniture was comfortable, yet elegant, in rich fabrics of velvet, leather, and linen.

The kitchen gave off a cozy, but airy feel with bright white cabinets and polished gleaming tile, paired with a natural wood table and sturdy chairs with Monet-type cushions. "Did you used to study art?" she asked.

Kennedy laughed and leaned against the counter. "Lord, no. But I'm obsessed with beauty in all forms. I love when things come together to please individuals in a visual and spiritual sense." She wrinkled her nose. "Wow, that sounded pompous."

"No, I know exactly what you mean! You were the one who put the photographs up in Connor's place, weren't you?"

"Guilty as charged. Connor is wonderful but decor is not one of his strong suits. Like most men, I'd have to say."

"Agreed."

"Now, let me ask you a question and you promise to give me an honest answer."

Ella swallowed. Her heart pounded furiously, and she prayed Kennedy didn't want to ask about her and Connor. About their relationship. She wanted to relax this afternoon and indulge in some girl chatter she'd been sorely lacking. She wanted fun and laughs and gossip, but not about her. "Of course." She held her breath.

"Do you really want coffee or can I just open up this bottle of wine? It's five o'clock somewhere."

Her shoulders slumped in relief. "Yes. No, I can do better than that. Hell, yes!"

Kennedy grinned and grabbed a corkscrew. "I knew I really liked you from the beginning. Are you excited for next week? It's makeover time."

She tapped her unpolished nail against the swirling gold granite. "I think. I'm nervous, though. I've always been a huge believer in appearances not being important."

"You sound exactly like Nate. I understand, but I don't agree. It's not about making you into someone you're not. It's about becoming a better you. Someone you like and can be comfortable with. I believe it's important to make a strong first impression and give yourself an opportunity to dive deeper. Make sense?"

Ella sighed. "I guess. Arilyn's counseling session was helpful, but I still have reservations about Luke adjusting to my dating. He's been so happy lately. I don't want to wreck anything."

Kennedy poured the Chardonnay into two glasses and slid one over to her. "I understand completely. But Luke also needs to see you taking care of yourself and being happy. You shouldn't have to deny that part of yourself in order to be a good mom. It's been two years, Ella. You're ready. We already found a fabulous match and Arilyn is working on getting a date set up."

She sipped her wine and tried hard not to think about Connor. "You're right. I'm definitely ready, and I'm excited to explore this new chapter."

Kennedy slid on a stool across from her and lifted her glass. "I know it's scary, but I promise you, it will be worth it. Sometimes we have to be brave enough to open up to someone new. Break out of our routine. Now, tell me about Connor."

She avoided her gaze. "What about him?"

Kennedy leaned in. "How bad are you torturing him in class?"

Ella smiled slowly. "Really bad. Gave him an extra credit project. A little Woolf. A dash of Brontë. And a dose of Austen. Hopefully it will teach him a bit of how far women have come and how we don't deserve to be called 'darlin' or 'pretty little thing.'"

Her new friend laughed with delight. "Finally! Do you know how hard it was to break Nate of his habit of saying the most awful things to women? I had to electrocute him with a buzzer to re-form his habits."

"You didn't."

Kennedy sighed. "Yeah. I did. At least it all worked out." She took another sip of wine. "See, the thing about Connor is besides being gorgeous and a bit clueless, he's got a great big heart that's just waiting for someone to keep it safe. He protected Nate when their household fell apart. He took care of him, put him through college, and never thought twice about himself. A man like that is special, even if you have to dig a bit deeper to unearth it. That's a man who you can count on for the long haul. Once he commits, he's all in."

Fascinated, she thought over the past weeks. The way he treated her son with a loving care that rocked her soul. His insistence on taking her car for an oil change, or fixing the backed up sink instead of calling the plumber. She remembered the roses on Valentine's Day, and the hours he spent with them on a Saturday night playing board games. "Why does he continue to date women who mean nothing to him?" she finally asked.

"I think we all get hurt and hide in certain ways. His way was removing any depth from his relationships. Then he'll always be safe."

Ella stared thoughtfully into the golden liquid, swirling it around the edge of the glass. The words shot straight and true across the counter and fired a direct hit. Kennedy was right. It was almost as if he was comfortable slipping into a role he rarely questioned. He smiled, flirted, and kept things light. He seemed to do the same thing on all his dates. Did he not know anymore how to allow himself to really feel? More importantly, did he even want to try?

"You're good at therapy, too. How do you see so much?"

"I spent years in therapy myself. I had issues galore. Still do. I learned one thing watching endless relationships begin, fail, break, and triumph." Kennedy lifted her glass in a mock salute. "You just have to find the right crazy for you."

Ella laughed and raised her own glass. "To the crazy."

They clicked glasses. And drank.

* * * *

A few hours and a bottle of wine later, Nate trudged inside, pressing a kiss to the top of Kennedy's head. Her hand automatically entwined with her lover in a rehearsed dance that had seeped into memory. A pang of envy hit Ella as she watched them, but it was a beautiful pang because it reminded her that type of love was out there.

"How's it going, ladies?" He raised a brow at the empty bottle of wine. "Good, I see."

"Very good," Kennedy affirmed. "You guys need a break? I've got some brownies for Luke."

"Did you bake them?" Nate asked.

Kennedy gave an affronted humph. "Of course not! I bought them at the bakery."

"Thank God. Then he'll love them."

Ella laughed. "There hasn't been a brownie Luke hasn't liked. I'm surprised they're still at it."

Nate faced her. He was a handsome man, with a sexy goatee emphasizing his sharp features, and gorgeous brown eyes with swirls of green. He was shorter and leaner than Connor, but the resemblance was immediate in the thrust of the nose, arched brow, and brightness of their eyes. "Luke is a wonderful kid, Ella. You should be really proud. Not only is he respectful, but he's a hard worker. Seems to have Connor's talent for woodworking."

"Thank you. Connor's great with Luke. They seem to have bonded."

Nate nodded, his gaze a bit foggy, like an absent-minded professor. "And with you," he said. "I've never seen my brother so happy."

She jerked in her seat. Trying to cover up her emotion, she jumped up. "Umm, I'm going to go check on them. Be right back."

"Take the side door," Kennedy said.

"Thanks." Ella headed down the hallway and out to the back deck, making her way down toward the newly framed shed. Her boots made no noise on the steps, and she heard the mingling of voices as she drew nearer. She was about to raise her voice and yell their names when she stopped cold, ears straining to hear more.

"Dad doesn't really care about me," her son was saying. Ella pressed her hand against her mouth, wishing she could teleport and kill her ex-husband for hurting Luke. "He's got this new woman now, and a new kid on the way. He doesn't need me anymore." His tone reflected an acceptance and bitterness a ten-year-old shouldn't have to know.

"That sucks, Luke. There's really nothing I can say to make it better either. I learned that myself when my own mother left me."

"What? Your mom left?" Luke asked in disbelief.

She heard the clanking of tools and then a deep sigh. "Yeah, it was pretty bad. I was only fourteen. She packed up her suitcases, and when I got home, she was gone. Never came back. Never called. It was like she decided she didn't want that type of life anymore so she left it behind. Along with me and Nate."

She blinked away the sting of tears and concentrated.

"What did you do? How—how did you get over it?"

"I didn't. But I needed to take care of my brother, and when my father began drinking and checked out, we were alone. Life went on. Even though I was sad and I missed my parents, I had Nate. I had friends. I had hope for a great big life I wasn't going to let anyone take from me. Does that make sense?"

Silence. Then a small voice. "Yeah. It does."

"Your dad may come back and ask for forgiveness later. He may not. But you have your mom, and with her on your side, you have more than a lot of kids today. Now, that's not going to make every day better, and you're still going to do stupid stuff like listening to the wrong boys or making huge mistakes. That's okay. You're a kid, you're supposed to screw up. The good news is your mom will be there to catch you every time. Just give her a break once in a while, okay? She likes that touchy feely stuff like hugs and it makes her happy."

Luke chuckled. She heard the shift of weight and another rattle behind the freshly formed shed wall. "Okay. I guess I can handle that."

"Cool. You did an awesome job, kid. Let's head back inside and see if we can wrestle up some sugar."

Ella backed slowly away, retreating into the shadows as they began to clean up.

Her hands shook, and her heart seemed to expand in her chest, breaking out of its limits and bursting in a frenzy of light prisms. She had done a terrible, awful, ridiculous thing.

She had fallen in love with Connor Dunkle.

Chapter Eleven

"I am not an angel,' I asserted; 'and I will not be one till I die: I will be myself.
Mr. Rochester, you must neither expect nor exact anything celestial of me - for you
will not get it, any more than I shall get it of you: which I do not at all
anticipate."—Charlotte Brontë, Jane Eyre

Connor checked his watch and hurriedly snapped the book closed.
Damn, he'd lost track of time. Shoving the book under a pile of
papers, he told himself it was completely acceptable to think *Jane Eyre*
did not suck. To his horror, he found it kind of hot. At least Brontë
didn't ramble on nonstop about being stuck in a room as a metaphor
for her life.

He'd never be a Woolf fan, no matter how hard Ella tried. But
over the weeks working on the paper, and being forced to research the
lives of the three authors she'd picked, he began to understand the
limits placed on creative females. A man could break the rules and be
called heroic. A woman was locked up in a mental institution or told to
shut up.

Heavy stuff.

He quickly brushed his teeth, changed his shirt, and headed next
door. Ella had her first big date set up by Kinnections and he was on
his first official babysitting night. He figured they'd order a pizza and
play some video games. Or maybe he'd let Luke rent the new Marvel
movie out on Pay-Per-View. He loved a good kick-butt superhero
movie.

He hadn't seen Ella since her makeover. Besides extra work shifts, he'd finally scored a meeting with management for an interview. With his solid reputation on the construction site and degree almost in hand, he'd exhibited confidence and felt good about his performance. All his hard work and preparation was finally paying off. He wondered if this was how Nate felt when he was hired at NASA. It was a heady feeling.

Connor didn't bother to knock. He let himself in and found Luke already playing his Wii. "Hey, dude. You up for pizza tonight?"

"Yeah! You up for me demolishing you in Super Smash Brothers tonight?"

He laughed. "You can certainly try. But I've been practicing. Where's your mom?"

"Upstairs getting ready. She even smells different. Perfume, I guess."

Unease trickled through him but he shrugged it off. He'd talked to Luke about his feelings seeing Ella dating, but the kid seemed solid. He hoped Kennedy had taken away the orange lipstick. It was easy for Connor to see past the surface and appreciate how amazing Ella was, but guys were still stuck on physical appearance. He hoped this guy treated her nicely and made her feel good about herself. She deserved it.

He headed to the kitchen to pour himself a glass of lemonade and turned around.

Then almost dropped the glass.

"How do I look?"

He stared. Speechless, his voice died in his throat and he could only look at the woman before him that was no longer Ella.

She was stunning.

Her hair had been cut and was finally out of the constricted bun. Glossy black waves tumbled over her shoulders and half covered one eye in a flirty manner. Where were her glasses? Instead, wide, dark eyes peered at him with a wariness he'd never seen before, almost as if she was vulnerable, waiting for his opinion. Without the thick frames, her eyes gleamed with gold, giving off an intensity that made shock waves tingle through him. Her face glowed in the low light, and her lips were full and lush, painted a deep, sexy red that contrasted dramatically with her dark hair and eyes.

But her body. Dear God. Her body...

A clingy red tank dipped low in the front and emphasized the full curves of her breasts. A trendy black jacket skimmed the lean lines of her body. Her skirt halted just short of her knee, showing off a tantalizing strip of bare skin before the leather of thigh high black boots began. His gaze dropped to her feet. The boots held a wicked heel that made him imagine all sorts of naughty things. A musky, earthy scent danced in the air and surrounded her, urging him to move closer and bury his nose against her skin.

Blistering heat surged through him. He was hard in seconds, aching to cross the room and touch her. This was not his Ella. This was some other woman bent on seduction and naughty games. What had Kennedy done to her?

She tugged at the jacket and clasped her arms nervously across her chest. The red tank slipped a bit lower, giving him a teasing glimpse of olive skin. "You don't like it. Oh, my God. Do I look like a slut? Kennedy told me to go in bold so I thought I'd take a chance. She helped me pick this out."

He tried to speak but he still hadn't found his voice. She waited, but when he was unable to utter a response, she gave a deep sigh and shook her head.

"Forget it. Just like a man to give no feedback. I'm not going to change. I spent a lot of money on this stupid outfit, and I can handle this. Listen, thanks for watching Luke tonight. I better go. I'm running late."

Finally, words emerged from his throat. His head spun like he'd gotten clobbered and little birdies were circling him. "You look, you look—great. Umm, maybe you'd be more comfortable in flats, though?"

She waved a manicured hand in the air. He caught the flash of scarlet red nails. "I practiced, I can handle it. Luke, sweetie, I love you. Listen to Connor and don't go to bed too late, okay?"

"Mom! You look beautiful!"

Her face lit up with pleasure. Why hadn't Connor told her that? Why was he acting so frikkin weird?

"Thanks, honey. That means a lot to me. Text me if there's any problem. See you later."

Her heels clicked on the floor and he followed. "Wait a minute. You're meeting him somewhere? Why isn't he picking you up? Don't you think that's kind of rude?"

Her red lips curved in a grin that was sexy as hell. "Come on, Dunkle, you've never picked up any of your dates, have you?"

He blanched. "That's different!"

"No, it's not. I feel safer meeting him at the restaurant, anyway."

She opened the door but he kept talking. "Be careful. He'll probably invite you up for a drink, but that's code for him trying to make a move."

She gave him a naughty wink. "Oh, goody. Maybe I'll be later than I thought."

"Ella!"

"Kidding, just kidding. Geez, calm down, Dad. I have done this before, you know."

"If you feel uncomfortable, call me. I'll come pick you up."

"I have my car, remember? Have you been working too hard? You're losing it."

His palms began to sweat. He fought the overwhelming urge to beg her not to go and stay home with him. They'd do their usual and hang out in sweats and play games and argue over Woolf. What if this guy tried to touch her? Was he kidding himself? What guy alive on the face of the earth would not want to touch her looking like this?

"Ella—wait—I—"

"Sorry, I gotta go. Have fun and thanks for this!"

She banged the door closed and left.

He stared through the window and watched her get into her car. The fabric of her skirt slid up even more, revealing a delicious path of skin that led all the way up to heaven. He should've told her to change. No, he couldn't do that. She needed to boost her confidence. But holy shit, that outfit should be illegal.

"Connor! Come on, let's play!"

Shaking off the fog, he sat next to Luke and grabbed a controller. He had no idea what he was doing, and at this point, he wasn't going to relax until she came back through that door.

This was going to be a long night.

* * * *

Ella sighed and counted down the minutes till she kicked off her shoes.

Being sexy was a lot of work. She'd been out of practice for a while, so maybe her body needed more time to adjust. Her toes were pinched by the high heels, and the leather snugly clasping her leg was making her itch. Her hair kept sliding into her face until she wished she had a few bobby pins to jam it up and forget it. The contacts she'd put in caused her eyes to dry, and she couldn't wait to pop them out and put on her glasses. And as usual, her lipstick had slid off within the hour, along with the rest of her makeup.

She pulled to the curb and cut the engine. Luke should be asleep by now. Dinner had been a long, relaxing affair with good conversation and expensive wine. She liked Ed. He was a professional, divorced dad who seemed to get the challenges she faced. They'd traded pictures of their kids, talked Common Core education, and discussed popular fiction. He was a big reader and knew Woolf. He was impressed with her career. He was nice.

And he invited her up for a drink afterward.

Ella had a hard time not laughing as she imagined Connor's face. She'd declined, and instead they strolled to the used bookstore in town and spent a pleasant hour shopping and sipping a cappuccino.

Ed asked to see her again. She'd agreed. It was the most positive, life affirming date she'd ever had because it reminded her she was a woman. A sexual woman. A woman who enjoyed a man's company and conversation. A woman who would eventually enjoy sex if she could just get there.

The only problem was Connor Dunkle.

Ella stared into the darkness, hands tapping the steering wheel. She kept seeing his face throughout the date. The way he'd stared at her in shock and gotten that hungry gleam of lust in his eyes. For her. She could practically feel the energy zinging between them, and she'd fought the impulse to cross the room and kiss him. She dreamed of feeling his lips just one more time over hers and his hands stroking her skin. She dreamed of him slamming her against the wall and taking her like a man possessed, hungry to slip between her thighs and claim her.

She squeezed her legs together as arousal hit. Why did she keep doing this to herself? She had to accept Connor was only a friend. She may have done something stupid and fallen for him, but it was her secret to keep. This date was the first step of her moving on. She may not have wanted to attack Ed across the table, but he'd made her feel good. Like there was hope.

She grabbed her purse and went inside. The house was quiet and halfway dark, so she tiptoed into the living room to see if they'd fallen asleep on the couch in front of the television.

"Did you have a good time?"

She jumped and spun around. Connor leaned against the wall in front of her, holding a beer. "You scared me! Is Luke in bed?"

"Yeah. We watched *Antman*, ate pizza, and he went to sleep an hour ago." His gaze narrowed, raking over her figure. Goose bumps broke out on her arms. "Did you have a good time?" he repeated.

She swallowed and walked past him, laying down her purse. "Yes. It was good. Thanks for watching him. I owe you."

She waited for him to say good night and head home, but he remained standing, oddly silent. Her stomach clenched and she nervously walked around the house, straightening odds and ends. Her skin burned as if he'd touched her, and tension cranked in the air around them. What was going on?

"Aren't you going to give me the details?" he drawled.

She put two cups in the dishwasher and opened up the refrigerator to snatch a bottle of water. "We had a nice dinner. He was a nice guy. Nothing much left to tell."

"Did he kiss you?"

She choked on the water and coughed uncontrollably. Anger replaced her nerves. "What kind of question is that? It's none of your business. I don't ask about your dates."

"But we're friends, right? Don't friends share all the juicy details?"

She raised her chin and glared. "We're not that type of friends, Connor. You're also still technically my student. Look, I don't know what's going on here, but I think you better leave."

He put the beer down on the counter. "You're right. I should leave." He squeezed his eyes shut as if an inner battle was being waged. "I don't want to mess this up. I should go home and forget everything I want to say to you right now. I should forget everything I want to do."

She stilled. Poised on the edge of heart-stopping danger, Ella knew the only way to escape unscathed was to tell him to leave one more time. He'd obey, and the next time they saw each other, they'd be back to friends. Instead, she sealed her fate. "What things?"

His eyes flew open. She waited for him to walk away. Instead, he strode toward her. Her breath whooshed out of her lungs as he stopped inches away, his beautiful face tight with concentration. The burning blue of his eyes scorched her. "Bad things. I've been thinking about you all night. About another man touching you. I hated it. I don't want to leave, and I don't want anyone else touching you, Ella."

Her body trembled. The leashed fury of lust and want flicked at her, and a low groan rose to her lips, a groan of pure need. Warning bells clanged. She desperately tried to think of all the reasons this was not a good idea, but her brain shut down and her body roared for more. "This isn't a good idea."

"No. This is a terrible idea, but I'm not in control. So you need to stop me. Because all night while you were on your date, I thought of touching you. Kissing you." He paused. "Fucking you."

"Oh, God." She practically shook at his dirty words, growing wet between her thighs. She lifted her arms to push him away, but instead they lay against his hard chest. The muscles jumped beneath her touch. "Connor."

He lowered his head. His breath struck her lips. "I don't want to hurt you. I don't want to screw up the best relationship I've ever had with a woman. But I want you, Ella. I want to put my hands all over you, under you, in you. I want to give you so much pleasure you can only say my name over and over. I know I should walk away, for both of our sakes. So, stop me, sweetheart. Stop me right now."

Their eyes met and locked. Her arms slid up over his chest and around his neck, and she rose to her tiptoes and said the words. "I can't. I don't want you to stop," she said softly. "Take what you want."

His mouth slammed over hers.

It was as if the months not touching had built up between them and exploded in a firestorm. Their first kiss in the snow had been so sweet and slow, a preliminary dance of exploration and growing arousal.

This kiss was raw lust and blistering need in a completely uncivilized world. He devoured her mouth whole, his tongue staking his claim, and he lifted her up in one swoop and placed her on the kitchen counter. Swallowing her throaty moans, he pushed open her legs and stood between them, his fingers gently caressing her cheek as his mouth worked its dirty magic.

Drunk on the taste and feel of him, she slipped her hands under his T-shirt and hit silky hard muscles and a nest of dense hair. Digging her fingernails into his flesh, he nipped at her bottom lip and ripped off her jacket, his erection pressing against her in mouth-watering temptation.

Ella lost her mind under his sensual assault. There were no rules between them as they tugged off clothes and worshipped bare skin. He yanked down her bra and sucked on her hard nipples, and she bit her lip to keep from screaming in pleasure. Her skirt was pushed up to her hips, and his fingers hooked under the lace of her panties and dove into her wet heat.

Her legs squeezed around his hips as he pumped his fingers in and out of her pussy, licking her nipple, and then he brushed the tight bud of her clit and she jerked in his arms.

"You feel so damn good," he muttered in her ear. "Wet and hot and sweet. I should take you to bed, go slow—"

"Right here, right now." She arched up as he teased her clit, his thumb rubbing in slow circles, driving her further. "Do you have a condom?"

He bit her neck, licked the hurt. Her fingers stumbled on the zipper of his jeans, but it finally opened and she pushed the denim over his hips. His hard, massive length sprung free, and she thanked heavens the man didn't wear underwear.

"Yes, in my pocket. Oh, God, you're going to come, aren't you? Come now. Come for me."

He pressed against her clit and plunged his fingers deep, curling just right.

She exploded, her hips jerking against him as she buried her mouth against his chest to muffle her scream. He cursed viciously and kept up the movements, wringing out her orgasm to a shattering conclusion.

He twisted his hands in her hair and kissed her fiercely. "Get the condom." Her voice came out husky, raspy. "I need you."

She squeezed his erection, working her fingers up and down his shaft until he threw back his head, eyes squeezed tight, his face carved in the lines of pure ecstasy. She drank in his expression, loving the pleasure she gave as her thumb skimmed the dripping tip and she increased the rhythm to a rapid pace, as he grew harder and longer under her touch.

He fumbled in his pocket and withdrew the condom. Ripping it open, she helped him sheathe himself, and then he pushed her back onto the counter and raised himself up, his arms resting on both sides of her body like a conqueror about to enjoy his spoils.

"I don't want to hurt you," he grit out. "I don't want to go fast."

She spread her legs wide and offered herself up. "Hurt me. Take me. Now."

He grasped her panties and tore. The material fell off, leaving her bare. He said her name, in a curse or a prayer, and surged inside her.

Ella gasped, embracing the raw edge of pain and pleasure as he filled her completely. Her body surrendered under his gentle hands, his rough thrusts that pushed her to the edge again, trembling under the force of earth-shattering tension and need.

She memorized every line of his face, every spark in his eyes. She gave him everything as he claimed her body and soul, and let herself fly with no other thought than to give in to the wracking waves of pleasure that claimed her body.

Gripping her hips and yanking her higher, he thrust even deeper, his fingers playing with her clit, and she whispered his name over and over as she came again.

"Yes, yes, fucking perfect. Fucking mine."

With a growl, he joined her, slamming his hips and taking her mouth in a deep, soul-stirring kiss.

Time paused. Their breathing slowed. Quiet fell.

Moving slowly, he removed and disposed of the condom, pulled up his jeans, and eased her gently to a sitting position. Ella watched in silence, not able to speak or think. He pulled down her skirt, eased up her jacket, and picked her up from the counter, walking into the living room.

Sitting down on the couch, he cuddled her on his lap and pulled the afghan over both of them. With a sigh, she laid her cheek against his chest, breathing in his scent. He stroked her hair and pressed his lips to the top of her head.

"I just want to hold you for a little while," he said quietly. "Is that okay?"

She held him tighter, snuggling into the warmth, and closed her eyes. "Yes."

Then she drifted to sleep.

Chapter Twelve

"Beauty was not everything. Beauty had this penalty — it came too readily, came too completely. It stilled life — froze it."—Virginia Woolf, To the Lighthouse

Connor stared at his test, trying to get his head in the game.

Cliché.

God, what had he done?

Her voice filled the classroom in a lilting melody that haunted him. She walked on soundless shoes, back and forth in front of the classroom, dressed in her usual attire. Long dark skirt. Black ballet-type slippers. A loose mid-sleeve sweater in a dull beige. Her hair was still up, but her bun wasn't as severe, and several silky locks escaped and pressed against her cheek. The glasses were back, sliding down her nose at regular intervals, and she used a scarlet-painted fingernail to jam them back in place. The orange lipstick was gone, replaced by a stained red that made it hard for him to concentrate on her words.

She was back to herself, but different. Everything had now changed. He knew how soft and silky her skin was underneath her clothes; knew the muscled strength of her legs as she wrapped them around his hips; knew how her tight, wet pussy clenched around him when he thrust inside her; knew the stinging bite of her teeth and the ripe fruit of her lips.

He'd spent all night imagining her kissing another guy. Imagining his friend, his Ella, belonging to someone else. He'd drank a beer and brooded, and soon he'd worked himself into such a state, when she came through the door he'd lost control.

He was wrecked. He couldn't stop thinking about that night, though three full days had passed without contact. He'd slipped away in the middle of the night, disentangling himself with her warm body. He thought about showing up at her door the next morning to talk. He thought about calling her. Instead, he took on back-to-back shifts, arriving home late, then spending hours on his homework.

He knew he'd see her today and planned to arrive early. Exchange a few words.

But he'd gotten caught in traffic and walked into class late. She hadn't even deigned to make a comment, keeping her gaze firmly averted and her focus on her lecture.

He was a monster. He'd slept with her and disappeared. She must despise him. This was the reason he didn't get involved with messy, raw emotions with women. This was the reason he stayed away from relationships and kept things light.

Nothing was light with Ella.

The big red C+ reflected his growing understanding of literature. What began as a boring, torturous class had evolved into a foray of thoughts and words that affected him. He'd finished *Jane Eyre*, tore through Brontë, and actually went back to find more of their work. They were nearing the end of the semester, and as long as he passed the final and turned in his extra credit paper, he'd graduate with honors.

Finally, she dismissed the class and he took the familiar path to her desk. He waited his turn while she spoke to some other students, and then the room emptied.

"What can I do for you today, Mr. Dunkle?"

He winced. Yeah, she was pissed. And she had every right to be. "Ella, I'm so sorry."

She studied him coldly. "This isn't the time nor the place. My classroom is reserved for academic questions. Is there a question you want to ask me, Mr. Dunkle?"

He jerked back, reminding himself she was right. He didn't want to get her in trouble. "No, Professor. I'm sorry to interrupt."

He walked out and did the only thing possible.

Waited until she was done.

He tracked her to her car and appeared in front of her. "Ella?"

She jumped, her hand at her throat. "You scared me! Why are you stalking me?" She looked around nervously. "We're still on campus. You may not care, but I don't want to put my son or my job at risk."

"I understand. Open the car."

She glared, but finally pressed the button. They got in the car, and he turned toward her. "I'm sorry," he repeated.

"Another apology? You seem to be good at them. Unfortunately, I'm unsure of what you're apologizing for. Leaving me in the middle of the night? Staying away for three days? Avoiding Luke? Or having sex with me?"

He winced and pushed his fingers through his hair in frustration. "None of it. All of it. I screwed up bad. I panicked because I didn't know where this would leave us. You and Luke mean the world to me and I couldn't keep my hands off you the other night. You deserve to hate me. I hate myself."

His honesty must have hit the right chords because she let out a deep breath and met his gaze. "Look, I was confused, too, but I don't regret it." Vulnerability gleamed in her eyes. "Do you?"

"No."

She nodded. She seemed to struggle with her emotions. He waited for her to share her confusion and admit her feelings for him. Instead, she gave him a tight smile.

"Good. I don't want us to act weird or avoid each other. It was an amazing night, and we'll just move on. Deal?"

His gut lurched. Why did she seem so eager to forget how amazing they were together? She didn't even seem interested in talking about their relationship. The sex had been the best he ever experienced. The level of heat and hunger she exhibited and released in him was almost primitive. He'd never felt such a deep connection. But she was smiling like he was a stranger and she was trying to be polite.

Irritation tingled his nerve endings. "Yeah. Fine. Deal. How about I come over and see Luke tonight?"

"He actually has a sleepover tonight."

"On a school night?"

"Yes, I gave him special permission. He's working on a science project with his two friends and the mother called to see if they could stay. I like these two boys, and I've met with Cathy for coffee. I figured it was good for him, and he promised he'd FaceTime with me."

"That's great." He paused, his heart pounding ridiculously in his chest. "Maybe you want to go out to eat tonight? Talk a bit more?"

Her gaze dropped from his and she stuck the key in her ignition. "Thanks, but I can't."

"Why?"

She dragged in a breath. "I have a date tonight."

His head was suddenly taken over by a swarm of angry bees. "With the same guy?"

"No, a new guy. Kennedy felt this new man would be a great match, and we both ended up free this evening."

"Oh." She'd been crying his name as he thrust inside her and now she was going to dinner with another man. This was what he wanted, right? He'd been afraid she'd get too serious on him and ruin their friendship. Things were back on the right track.

Cliché.

"Great. Hope you have a good time." He reached for the door handle.

"Connor?"

"What?"

Her voice was whisper soft. "This is what you want, right? For us to move on with other people?"

Tension drew his body taut. His heart did a strange flip-flop, screaming for him to change the rules. Tell her he didn't want her to date anyone else. Admit he was scared but wanted to see where this could go.

"Yes. I think it's good for both of us."

She paused. "Okay."

"Have a good time tonight."

He left the car without another word, wondering why the hell he was so pissed off.

And what he could do about it.

* * * *

That night, he watched from behind his curtains as she left on her date. Tonight, she wore silky black pants that clung to her magnificent ass, spiked heels, and a lacey black top that looked like it wasn't enough material to go out in public with.

He fumed and waited. Drank a beer and waited some more. Tried to do homework, watch television, or read a book.

And waited some more.

A few hours later, her car pulled up to the curb and she got out. He watched her head toward her apartment, then pause in front of his door. Connor held his breath, his palm pressed to the cool windowpane. She glanced over, as if sensing his presence. She turned, stopped, and closed her eyes as if in an inner battle with herself.

Come to me, he mentally urged. His body tensed, waiting for her next move. Waiting for her decision. *Come to me, Ella.*

Her lips parted and she mouthed a familiar curse word she loved but rarely uttered. Then headed toward him.

He met her halfway. Just opened the door, dragged her inside, and took her in his arms. She never hesitated, lifting her mouth for his kiss, the earthy, musky scent of her curling in his nostrils. He was ravenous, rock hard in seconds, and his brain repeated one word over and over again without pause.

Mine.

He possessed her mouth with all the pent-up arousal and frustration racing through his body. Without speaking, he lifted her and walked into his bedroom, laying her down on the navy blue comforter.

"I waited for you," he finally said. He took in the spill of her dark hair over his pillow, the rapid breath raising her breasts, the long lines of her legs spread open.

"I know," she said huskily.

"You are so damn beautiful."

She blinked, raised her arms, and he crawled on the bed. Clothes drifting off, he worshipped her, spreading her out, touching and tasting every precious inch of flesh. He buried his mouth between her legs and drank in her essence, his tongue swiping her hardened clit, gripping her writhing body and bringing her to orgasm while he drank in every spasm and demanded more, always more.

Fitting himself with a condom, he rolled and lifted her over him.

She took him deep, rocking her hips to a wicked, eternal rhythm, her breasts spilling into his hands as he rubbed her tight nipples and let her set the pace.

When his orgasm came, the brutal pleasure shook him to the core, diving deep into places of his soul he never knew existed and giving it all over to her. He swallowed her screams as she shattered around him, and Connor held her tight afterward, knowing he may not be able to let her go again.

Chapter Thirteen

"A person can't have everything in this world; and it was a little unreasonable of her to expect it."—Kate Chopin, The Kiss

"I have to go."

A full moon hung ripe in the sky. She sat on the edge of the bed, looking out the slats of the blinds, realizing she couldn't do this anymore.

She had wanted to try. God, she wanted him that badly. She'd gone on that date, made polite conversation, laughed at his jokes, allowed his touch on her elbow as he guided her to the car, and thought about Connor Dunkle. Her date promised to call and she agreed to go out with him again, and then she drove home and knocked on Connor's door.

He'd been waiting for her. Somehow, deep inside, she'd known. She wanted to convince herself she'd be able to engage in a hot affair with her next-door neighbor and her friend. She swore she'd be able to keep it light, realizing he was the type of man who didn't look for long term and liked his easygoing, uncommitted lifestyle.

Instead, she'd fallen in love with him. And she wasn't going to pretend any longer.

"Don't go." He rolled over and rubbed her shoulders. Pressed a kiss to the nape of her neck. "Stay with me."

"Why?"

His grip tightened. "Because I want more time."

Ella took a deep breath and stood. She felt his gaze on her as she pulled on her clothes, and he kept silent until she faced him. "How is this going to work, Connor?" she asked with a lightness she didn't feel. "Are we going to have sex each time I come home from a date? What's the term everyone uses? Fuck buddies?"

He flew up from the bed and stood before her, naked. His voice was a low growl of sound. "Don't you ever use that term about us," he bit out. "You're important to me."

"And you're important to me. But we've crossed over into new territory and I've been afraid to scare you off. I can't pretend I don't have these feelings for you while I date other men. So, I'm going to ask, what do you want?"

He blinked. Stared at her. "I want you."

She nodded. "In a committed, long-term relationship?" she asked calmly.

The look on his face told the truth. Sheer panic lit up those blue eyes, and he turned quickly away, as if to buy more time. "I thought—I thought we'd just take it slow. See how things go."

Her heart shriveled but Ella needed to see the whole thing to the end. She owed both of them the truth.

"I understand," she said softly. "I really do. But I can't play those types of games. See, I'm in love with you."

He flinched. Tore his fingers through his hair. Stared at her as if she'd sprouted wings and was about to fly off into the night like some alien creature. "What?"

She fought the pain and humiliation, raising her chin. "I love you. Crazy, right? I'll tell you this—I never expected to fall for a man like you. You were right when you told me I had made judgments. I thought you were a chauvinistic, egotistical, shallow man out for a good lay and a good time. Instead, I discovered you have a beautiful heart, and mind, and soul. You treat Luke like your own. You rose above odds so many others couldn't and made a life for you and your brother. You're kind and giving, loyal, and wicked smart. You're everything I've always dreamed of."

He shook his head as if trying to register her words. "Ella, I don't know what to say. I'm crazy about you, but we just started this, and it happened kind of fast, and I don't want to hurt Luke or you. I don't want to hurt anyone."

As she studied him, the light bulb exploded and shattered in tiny, jagged pieces. She pressed her hand to her mouth as a bitter, humorless laugh left her lips. Now she understood.

"My God, I get it. You only made a move because I changed my appearance. I wasn't enough for you physically before that, was I? You just liked who I became when I pretended to be like all the other women you date. I bet if I hadn't gone out with Ed, you would've never tried to kiss me or take me to bed. Suddenly, it was easier for you, wasn't it? Less of a risk."

"That's ridiculous. I don't know what you're talking about."

But the truth was revealed in his face, and anger bubbled up like lava, whipping her into a frenzy. "Oh, yes you do. As long as I was dressing plain and not up to your sexual standards, I was safe. Easy to stay away from, huh? But the moment you got tricked with what I could look like, you had to make a move. You haven't changed at all. And I was an idiot to think I was special to you."

He closed the distance and grabbed her arms with a fierceness that challenged her own. "You are special! Don't ever talk about yourself like that. I always thought you were beautiful."

"I call bullshit." She jerked away. "You know what you think is beautiful, Connor? This." She tugged at the form-fitting lace top. "Fancy clothes and sexy heels." She fisted her hair and shook the waves wildly. "Perfectly tousled hair and red lipstick and perfume that makes you think of sex. It's easier, isn't it? But guess what? It's all a mirage. One morning, or one day, or one year, you wake up and find this." She swept her hands over her body with emphasis. "You get glasses and sweats and messy hair and a bare face. You get just me, with no fancy trappings. You get real. And I was crazy to think you were ready for it."

Waves of anger and frustration emanated from his figure. "I don't know what I'm ready for!" he yelled. "I know I'm crazy about you and Luke and that my feelings have changed since I walked in your class that first day, and I'm not sure what to do about it. I don't give a shit about your appearance. Can't you see I'm nuts about you? I can get real!"

She wrapped her arms around her chest and shook her head. "No. I just know I can't do this with you. I'm looking for a relationship, not just sex. I'm looking for a man I can grow old with and who wants to be a father to my son. How's that for real?"

"You don't want to give me a chance here? Let me catch up. Think about how this will work and what I can offer you?"

She smiled sadly. "Your answer said enough, Connor. I have to go."

"What about us? What about Luke?"

Her heart ached but she forced herself to speak. "Luke adores you and I'd never say you can't see him. Just—just give me some time, okay? I think we need a break."

"I don't want to hurt you, Ella."

"I know," she said. "When you open yourself up to love someone, there's no way not to get hurt. You just have to decide if it's worth the pain."

Ella left him alone in his bedroom, wondering if he could hear the sound of her heart shattering.

* * * *

"You look like shit."

Connor lifted his beer mug and stared moodily at his brother. They'd agreed to meet at the pub downtown. Nate held his usual cocktail, a Darth Maultini, but Connor wasn't even in the mood to tease him about it.

The semester was coming to an end. Luke continued to come over to his house and do homework, but Connor made sure to cite work as an excuse to stay away from Ella. Class became a torturous session that tore him apart. He ached to touch her. Talk to her. Insist they were being ridiculous by not trying to be together.

But he realized, deep down, Ella was right.

He hadn't made a move until she walked in that kitchen transformed. When he looked back on their first kiss in the snow, he remembered keeping a lock-down on his hormones and emotions. He'd treated her more carefully, with more respect. The moment she came at him in a low-cut top and short skirt, and he thought of her kissing some guy, he'd lost his control. Somehow, it seemed safer to play with a sexually experienced, hot woman. He knew the rules.

God, he was such an ass.

"Yeah, it's been a tough few weeks. How's Kennedy?"

"Hard-headed as usual. She found her engagement ring and kind of freaked out."

He almost spit out his beer. "Dude, are you serious? You asked her to marry you?"

Nate waved a hand carelessly in the air. "I ask her to marry me all the time. The ring is for the formal asking I'm planning for her. Of course, she stumbled across it and majorly lost her mind. This may be the hardest woman in the world to pin down."

"Why can't you just leave things alone?" he asked in frustration. "You're both happy. Shacked up. Who needs marriage?"

Nate looked surprised. "I do. I love her. She wants to get married, too, but the woman is stubborn. Eventually I'll get her to agree. How's Ella?"

He grunted. "Fine."

"Luke?"

"Fine."

"How's school? Graduation is May, right?"

"Yep, I'm all set. As long as I pass Ella's class."

"And work? You still going for that big management position?"

"Yep. They offered me the job."

Nate laughed with delight. "Congratulations! Not that I'm surprised, but damn, I'm proud of you."

"Thanks."

He tried to force a happy smile, but he was too miserable. Nate stared at him hard, his green eyes seeing way too much, like he always did. He tapped a finger against the edge of the table in a steady rhythm. "You're in love with Ella, aren't you?"

Connor jerked back, splashing beer over the rim of his glass. "Holy shit, dude, why'd you ask me a question like that?"

His brother shrugged. "I could tell. You're a mess. Something happened between you two. Just tell me."

So Connor did. He told Nate the entire story from start to finish, and Ella's expectations, and his confusion, and dumped it all out in one long, messy stream of words. There was no one else he trusted more in the world than Nate. His brother took it all in with that quiet manner, just nodding here and there as he urged him to continue.

Finally, he fell silent. The cocktail waitress took that moment to slide by their table and smile cheerily. "Can I get you another round, gentlemen?"

He automatically switched into gear, giving her a big smile and wink. "We'll have anything you're giving, sweetheart."

She giggled and cocked her head in a flirty manner. "Oh, yeah? I may have to take you up on that offer later."

"I'll be waiting. For now, I think we're good."

With another sidelong look, she walked away with an extra swing of her hips that did nothing for him. When he turned back to his brother, Nate was looking at him in pure shock.

"You're unbelievable. That was the stupidest, most asinine pick-up line I ever heard. And she fell for it! You're the only guy I know who gets away with that behavior. No wonder you're such an ass. Women have been falling for you your whole life and you've never had to work hard to really keep one."

Connor's mouth fell open. "That's a shitty thing to say to me! I just poured out my heart and you're giving me a hard time because the waitress liked me?"

Nate dropped his face into his hands and groaned. "God, you're just like Kennedy. I swear, it's scary. You both have intimacy issues. You're both stuck on stupid images and your ideas of beauty. You're both terrified of being left alone and getting your heart broken. You both are driving me nuts."

Shock poured through him. "I'm not afraid of being left. I've always broken up with women, not the other way around. Is it wrong to accept the truth about myself? I'm not meant for long-term or serious relationships. I'm not built that way."

Nate looked up and stared at him with serious eyes. "Connor, I need you to listen to me, man. You were left in the most devastating way possible. Mom left you. Oh, you always talked about how hard it was on me, but you're the one who got stuck with all the crap. You watched Dad take off and had to raise me. You had to be the parent in the relationship, and you never got the answers of why. Then you got this stupid idea that you had no brains, like the intelligence was distributed only to one family member, and you limited yourself."

His stomach lurched at the mention of Mom. He hated thinking about it, but Nate held his attention and he knew it was important to listen.

"I think you built this whole image of yourself because it was easier. Women flocked to you, so you gave them what they expected, and along the way, you lost who you really are. Dude, you're graduating with honors from college. You work on the fucking Tappan Zee Bridge, you're a master in construction, and now management hired you for their team. I saw you with Luke. He adores you, and that doesn't surprise me in the least. You're great with kids, and you'd be the best father in the world."

Raw emotion cut at him like tiny paper cuts. He wanted to duck his head, walk away, and not deal with his brother's speech, but he kept still and let himself really hear his brother for the first time.

"Ella sees everything in you that we all see, except for you. The only reason you let yourself make a move on her wasn't because she suddenly appeared in a skirt and heels. It was because you finally gave yourself permission. You took a chance. But then you spooked and backed off and tried to make yourself think it was better this way. It's not, Connor. You love Ella. You love Luke. Just let yourself love them, man, and take a shot. What do you really have to lose? A life of loneliness? A life filled with shallow encounters that never scratch the surface? You're worth more than that."

As his brother's words washed over him, his body came to life. The shaking started deep inside and spread throughout his body until the most ridiculous thing began to happen.

Tears stung his eyes.

Oh, fuck no. Not here. He absolutely refused to cry like a pussy in front of his brother in a bar.

Instead, he rubbed his face, took another swig of beer, and cleared his throat. "Okay."

Nate nodded and sipped at his god-awful feminine cocktail. "Okay."

A mixture of peace and acceptance flowed through him. His brother was right. He'd made a mistake, but it wasn't too late yet. He owed them both a chance to fix the wrongs and fight for something he wanted.

He sat with his brother in companionable silence and drank.

Chapter Fourteen

"...who shall measure the heat and violence of a poet's heart when caught and tangled in a woman's body?"—Virginia Woolf, A Room of One's Own

Ella clasped her hands on top of her desk and swept her gaze over the classroom. Students scribbled furiously, occasionally sneaking glances at the clock. The familiar sounds of low mutters, chairs creaking, and deep sighs echoed in the air. Final exams stressed everyone out, but she was positive she'd done her job and every single student would pass.

Even Connor Dunkle.

Her gaze settled on him for a heart-stopping instant. Those golden locks spilled over his forehead, and his brow was creased in concentration. He wrote in a frenzy, fingers gripped around his pen like a vise, concentration evident in the tight lines of his face.

It had been a week since their night together. Each day was painful, but Ella reminded herself it was better to heal now. At least Luke never got attached to the concept of them as a couple. At least she was the only casualty this time.

A sigh shuddered through her. After the anger passed, only a dull resignation settled in like a bad bruise. Connor had never pretended to be different. He hadn't promised her a future or even a tomorrow. Oh, she knew he cared about her, but he hadn't tumbled into love like she had. Eventually, she'd heal and hopefully they could remain friends. Maybe, with time, she'd be able to look into his face without craving to touch him.

Maybe not.

One by one, students finished their exam and dropped it off at her desk, gathered up their stuff and left. The end of the semester was always bittersweet. It reminded her of the passing of time, the growth of her students, and the hope she'd made a slight difference. Her love of literature was a part of her, and if she'd converted just one more person to recognize the beauty of the authors she taught, Ella considered it a life well lived.

"Time's up," she announced. Four students remained. She waited while they trudged over, dropping their papers, saying good-bye, and then leaving.

Connor remained behind.

Ella prayed he'd let her be. She was still too raw, like an oozing, open wound refusing to scab. Slowly, he unfurled his length from the chair and walked to her desk. Laid the exam in front of her. Then handed her a stack of papers neatly bound in a folder.

"I finished my extra credit project."

She nodded, her throat thick with emotion. "Congratulations. I'll grade it quickly and make sure I send the Registrar your grade so you can prepare for graduation. I have no doubt you did well on the final. You've been working hard."

"Ella. There's so much I want to say to you."

"Don't." Her voice broke and she let out a small laugh. "You don't, you don't need to say anything."

"I'm asking you to do one thing for me. Read my paper when you get home tonight. I need your feedback."

"Connor, I'm sure you did a great job."

"Read it. Tonight. Promise me?"

She gave a jerky nod, unable to speak. Those ocean-blue eyes raked over her face and down her body in a caress, blazing with intensity that made her shake. Then he was gone.

Ella buried her face in her hands. At least she didn't have to see him in class any longer. That would help.

She picked up the folder and skimmed through it. Neatly typed, with a full bibliography and references, it looked to be perfectly acceptable. She tossed it in the pile and got ready for her next class.

Hours later, she drove home, made dinner, and climbed into her pajamas. Luke had been in a good mood, chattering about school and his two new friends, and she savored his happiness, allowing it to fill her up and soothe her pain. He went upstairs to shower and get ready for bed, and Ella decided to make a cup of tea and curl up on the sofa with a book.

As she made her tea, her gaze fell on her briefcase. Why was Connor so insistent she read his paper tonight? Was he really worried she wouldn't pass him? A tingle of awareness flowed through her. With a sigh, she retrieved his paper, a red pen, and sat down with her tea. Better to read it now and let him know or he'd worry.

Time ticked. She flipped pages, jotting down notes and growing more impressed by the depth of the work. It was obvious he wasn't crazy about *To the Lighthouse,* but he seemed to embrace *Jane Eyre* and *Pride and Prejudice.* A smile rested on her lips. He was a closet romantic and didn't realize it. His overall insights to *A Room of One's Own* startled her with depth. He'd stripped away his usual mockery of whining women and connected with the isolation and dedication a woman writer had to face; the solitude and willingness to dive deep in order to unearth the emotions needed to bleed on the page.

A dull ache settled into her bones as she reached the end. God, she missed him. It was as if he was right here next to her while she read his voice on the page. Ella began to close the folder when her fingers skated over one last paper.

A letter.

She sucked in her breath. A letter handwritten to her, the personal scrawl filling up the page. She closed her eyes. Could she do this right now? Was she ready to hear things that would only hurt her deeper?

Ella began to read.

Dear Ella,

You were right. When we first met, it was easy to resist you. Besides being a pain in the ass, failing me in class, and finding out you were my new next-door neighbor, I wasn't truly prepared to think of you in any romantic way. When I bonded with Luke, I realized what a wonderful mother you were. When you insisted on pushing my limits in class, I realized what a wonderful teacher you were. When you challenged me to get real, I realized what a wonderful woman you were.

But you were also wrong. It wasn't your image, or clothes, or perfume that finally made me surrender to my need to touch you. I had been searching for you my entire life, but I didn't know it yet. Unfortunately, what I had been searching for I was also terrified of finding. It was easier to hide with shallow relationships and believe in a stereotype I'd been taught my entire life.

That I wasn't worth loving.

You taught me I am. You taught me to stop settling and relying on my surface qualities to skate through life without injury. You taught me there was something greater to fight for, but once again, my insecurities and fear allowed me to let you walk away.

I love the way you scrunch up your nose when you're irritated. I love the way you giggle when Luke tells those terrible knock-knock jokes, and I love your awful meatloaf you still insist on serving, and I love the way you defend the beauty of Virginia Woolf, and I love those ugly sweaters you wear, and the beautiful body and heart and soul that beats true beneath your clothes.

I love you, Ella Blake. I love your son. You're the only woman I want, and I'm going to spend the rest of my life convincing you I'm worth taking a second chance on.

Open your door.

Connor

She didn't hesitate. The decision had been made the moment his soul-stirring words lifted from the paper and arrowed straight through to her heart. She rose from the couch, walked across the room, and opened the door.

He stood before her clutching a bouquet of red roses.

"Will you be mine, Ella Blake?"

She gazed at his beloved face and the way his eyes told her the truth, gleaming in the depths of a bottomless ocean blue.

"I already was," she said simply.

She stepped into his arms and he kissed her, long and slow and sweet. When he lifted his head, Ella smiled.

"You officially passed my class. Congratulations."

He laughed and swung her up high, holding her close, and Ella realized they'd both found what they were searching for and more.

The End

Sign up for the 1001 Dark Nights Newsletter
and be entered to win a Tiffany Key necklace.

There's a contest every month!

Go to www.1001DarkNights.com to subscribe.

As a bonus, all subscribers will receive a free
1001 Dark Nights story
The First Night
by Lexi Blake & M.J. Rose

Turn the page for a full list of the
1001 Dark Nights fabulous novellas...

Discover 1001 Dark Nights Collection Three

HIDDEN INK by Carrie Ann Ryan
A Montgomery Ink Novella

BLOOD ON THE BAYOU by Heather Graham
A Cafferty & Quinn Novella

SEARCHING FOR MINE by Jennifer Probst
A Searching For Novella

DANCE OF DESIRE by Christopher Rice

ROUGH RHYTHM by Tessa Bailey
A Made In Jersey Novella

DEVOTED by Lexi Blake
A Masters and Mercenaries Novella

Z by Larissa Ione
A Demonica Underworld Novella

FALLING UNDER YOU by Laurelin Paige
A Fixed Trilogy Novella

EASY FOR KEEPS by Kristen Proby
A Boudreaux Novella

UNCHAINED by Elisabeth Naughton
An Eternal Guardians Novella

HARD TO SERVE by Laura Kaye
A Hard Ink Novella

DRAGON FEVER by Donna Grant
A Dark Kings Novella

KAYDEN/SIMON by Alexandra Ivy/Laura Wright
A Bayou Heat Novella

STRUNG UP by Lorelei James
A Blacktop Cowboys® Novella

MIDNIGHT UNTAMED by Lara Adrian
A Midnight Breed Novella

TRICKED by Rebecca Zanetti
A Dark Protectors Novella

DIRTY WICKED by Shayla Black
A Wicked Lovers Novella

A SEDUCTIVE INVITATION by Lauren Blakely
A Seductive Nights New York Novella

SWEET SURRENDER by Liliana Hart
A MacKenzie Family Novella

For more information, visit www.1001DarkNights.com

Discover 1001 Dark Nights Collection One

Also from 1001 Dark Nights

For more information, visit www.1001DarkNights.com

Discover 1001 Dark Nights Collection Two

Also from 1001 Dark Nights

For more information, visit www.1001DarkNights.com

About Jennifer Probst

Jennifer Probst is the *New York Times*, *USA Today*, and *Wall Street Journal* bestselling author of both sexy and erotic contemporary romance. She was thrilled her novel, *The Marriage Bargain*, was the #6 Bestselling Book on Amazon for 2012, and spent 26 weeks on the *New York Times*. Her work has been translated in over a dozen countries, sold over a million copies, and was dubbed a "romance phenom" by Kirkus Reviews. She makes her home in New York with her sons, husband, two rescue dogs, and a house that never seems to be clean. She loves hearing from all readers! Stop by her website at http://www.jenniferprobst.com for all her upcoming releases, news and street team information. Sign up for her newsletter at www.jenniferprobst.com/newsletter for a chance to win a gift card each month and receive exclusive material and giveaways.

Everywhere and Every Way

The Billionaire Builders
by Jennifer Probst
May 31, 2016

Hot on the heels of her beloved Marriage to a Billionaire novels, *New York Times* bestselling author Jennifer Probst nails it with the first in an all-new sexy romance series featuring red-hot contractor siblings who give the Property Brothers a run for their money!

Ever the responsible eldest brother, Caleb Pierce started working for his father's luxury contracting business at a young age, dreaming of one day sitting in the boss's chair. But his father's will throws a wrench in his plans by stipulating that Caleb share control of the family business with his two estranged brothers.

Things only get more complicated when demanding high-end home designer Morgan hires Caleb to build her a customized dream house that matches her specifications to a T—or she'll use her powerful connections to poison the Pierce brothers' reputation. Not one to ignore a challenge, Caleb vows to get the job done—if only he can stop getting distracted by his new client's perfect...amenities.

But there's more to icy Morgan than meets the eye. And Caleb's not the only one who knows how to use a stud-finder. In fact, Morgan is pretty sure she's found hers—and he looks quite enticing in a hard hat. As sparks fly between Morgan and Caleb despite his best intentions not to mix business and pleasure, will she finally warm up and help him lay the foundation for everlasting love?

* * * *

Prologue

Caleb Pierce craved a cold beer, air-conditioning, his dogs, and maybe a pretty brunette to warm his bed.

Instead, he got lukewarm water, choking heat, his head in an earsplitting vice, and a raging bitch testing his temper.

And it was only eight a.m.

"I told you a thousand times I wanted the bedroom for my mother off the garage." Lucy Weatherspoon jabbed her French-manicured finger at the framing and back at the plans they'd changed twelve times. "I need her to have privacy and her own entrance. If this is the garage, why is the bedroom off the other side?"

He reminded himself again that running your own company had its challenges. One of them was clients who thought building a house was like shopping at the mall. Sure, he was used to difficult clients, but Lucy tested even his patience. She spoke to him as if he was a bit dim-witted just because he wore jeans with holes in them and battered work boots and had dust covering every inch of his body. His gut had told him to turn down the damn job of building her dream house, but his stubborn father overruled him, calling her congressman husband and telling him Pierce Brothers would be fucking *thrilled* to take on the project. His father always did have a soft spot for power. Probably figured the politician would owe him a favor.

Yeah, Cal would rather have a horse head in his bed than deal with Congressman Weatherspoon's wife.

He wiped the sweat off his brow, noting the slight wrinkle of her nose telling him he smelled. For fun, he deliberately took a step closer to her. "Mrs. Weatherspoon, we went over this several times, and I had you sign off. Remember? Your mother's bedroom has to be on the other side of the house because you decided you wanted the billiard room to be accessed from the garage. Of course, I can add it to the second floor with a private entry, but we'd need to deal with a staircase or elevator."

"No. I want it on the ground floor. I don't remember signing off on this. Are you telling me I need to choose between my mother and the pool table room?"

He tried hard not to gnash his teeth. He'd already lost too much of the enamel, and they'd just broken ground on this job. "No. I'm saying if we put the bedroom on the other side of the house, it won't break the architectural lines, and you can have everything you want. Just. Like. We. Discussed."

She tapped her nude high-heeled foot, studying him as if trying to decipher whether he was a sarcastic asshole or just didn't understand how to talk to the natives. He gave his best dumb look, and finally she sighed. "Fine. I'll bend on this."

Oh, goody.

"But I changed my mind on the multilevel deck. I found this picture on Houzz and want you to recreate it." She shoved a glossy printout of some Arizona-inspired massive patio that was surrounded by a desert. And yep, just as he figured, it was from a spa hotel, which looked nothing like the lake-view property he was currently building on. Knowing it would look ridiculous on the elegant colonial that rivaled a Southern plantation, he forced himself to nod and pretend to study the picture.

"Yes, we can definitely discuss this. Since the deck won't affect my current framing, let's revisit when we begin designing the outside."

That placated her enough to get her to smile stiffly. "Very well. Oh, I'd better go. I'm late for the charity breakfast. I'll check in with you later, Caleb."

"Great." He nodded as she picked her way carefully over the building site and watched her pull away in her shiny black Mercedes. Cal shook his head and gulped down a long drink of water, then wiped his mouth with the back of his hand. Next time, he'd get his architect Brady to deal with her. He was good at charming an endless array of women when they drew up plans, but was never around to handle the temper tantrums on the actual job.

Then again, Brady had always been smarter than him.

Cal did a walk-through to check on his team. The pounding sounds of classic Aerosmith blared from an ancient radio that had nothing on those fancy iPods. It had been on hundreds of jobs with him, covered in grime, soaked with water, battered by falls, and never stopped working. Sure, when he ran, he liked those wireless contraptions, but Cal always felt as if he was born a few decades too late. To him, simple was better. Simple worked just fine, but the more houses he built, the more he was surrounded by requests for fancier equipment, for endless rooms that would never be used, and for him to clear land better left alone.

He nodded to Jason, who was currently finishing up the framing, and ran his hand over the wood, checking for stability and texture. His hands were an extension of all his senses, able to figure out weak spots hidden in rotted wood or irregular length. Of course, he wasn't as gifted as his youngest brother, Dalton, who'd been dubbed the Wood Whisperer. His middle brother, Tristan, only laughed and suggested wood be changed to *woody* to be more accurate. He'd always been the wiseass out of all of them.

Cal wiped the thought of his brothers out of his head, readjusted his hard hat, and continued his quick walk-through. In the past year, Pierce Brothers Construction had grown, but Cal refused to sacrifice quality over his father's constant need to be the biggest firm in the Northeast.

On cue, his phone shrieked, and he punched the button. "Yeah?"

"Cal? Something happened."

The usually calm voice of his assistant, Sydney, broke over the line. In that moment, he knew deep in his gut that everything would change: like the flash of knowledge before a car crash, or the sharp cut of pain before a loss penetrated the brain. Cal tightened his grip on the phone and waited. The heat of the morning pressed over him. The bright blue sky, streaked with clouds, blurred his vision. The sounds of Aerosmith, drills, and hammers filled his ears.

"Your father had a heart attack. He's at Haddington Memorial."

"Is he okay?"

Sydney paused. The silence told him everything he needed to know and dreaded to hear. "You need to get there quick."

"On my way."

Calling out quickly to his team, he ripped off his hat, jumped into his truck, and drove.

* * * *

A mass of machines beeped, and Cal tried not to focus on the tubes running into his father's body in an attempt to keep him alive. They'd tried to keep him out by siccing security on him and making a scene, but he refused to leave until they allowed him to stand beside his bed while they prepped him for surgery.

Christian Pierce was a hard, fierce man with a force that pushed through both opposition and people like a tank. At seventy years old, he'd only grown more grizzled, in both body and spirit, leaving fear and respect in his wake but little tenderness. Cal stared into his pale face while the machines moved up and down to keep breath in his lungs and reached out tentatively to take his father's hand.

"Get off me, for God's sake. I'm not dying. Not yet."

Cal jerked away. His father's eyes flew open. The familiar coffee-brown eyes held a hint of disdain at his son's weakness, even though they were red rimmed and weary. Cal shoved down the brief flare of pain and arranged his face to a neutral expression. "Good, because I want you to take over the Weatherspoons. They're a pain in my ass."

His father grunted. "I need some future political favors. Handle it." He practically spit at the nurse hovering and checking his vitals. "Stop poking me. When do I get out of here?"

The pretty blonde hesitated. Uh-oh. His father was the worst patient in the world, and he bit faster than a rattlesnake when cornered. Already, he looked set to viciously tear her to verbal pieces while she seemed to be gathering the right words to say.

Cal saved her by answering. "You're not. Doctor said you need surgery to unblock some valves. They're sending you now."

His father grunted. "Idiot doctor has been wanting me to go under the knife for years. He just wants to make money and shut me up. He's still bitching I overcharged him on materials for his house."

"You did."

"He can afford it."

Cal didn't argue. He knew the next five minutes were vital, before his father was wheeled into surgery. He'd already been told by the serious-faced Dr. Wang that it wouldn't be an easy surgery. Not with his father's previous heart damage from the last attack and the way he'd treated his body in the past few years. Christian liked his whiskey, his cigars, and his privacy. He thought eating healthy and walking on treadmills were for weaklings. When he was actually doing the construction part of the business, he'd been in better shape, but the last decade his father had faded to the office work and wheeling and dealing behind the scenes.

"I'm calling Tristan and Dalton. They need to know."

In seconds, his father raged at him in pure fury. "You will not. Touch that fucking phone and I'll wipe you out of my will."

Cal gave him a hard stare, refusing to flinch. "Go ahead. Been looking to work at Starbucks anyway."

"Don't mock me. I don't want to deal with their guilt or bullshit.

I'll be fine, and we both know it."

"Dad, they have a right to know."

"They walked out on me. They have a right to know nothing." A thin stream of drool trickled from his mouth. Cal studied the slow trek, embarrassed his father couldn't control it. Losing bodily functions would be worse than death for his father. He needed to come out of this surgery in one whole piece, or he didn't know what would happen.

Ah, shit, he needed to call his brothers. His father made a mule look yogic. They might have had a falling-out, and not spoken for too long, but they were still family. The hell with it. He'd contact them as soon as his father went into surgery—it was the right thing to do.

Christian half rose from the pillow. "Don't even think about going behind my back, boy. I have ways of making your life hell beyond the grave, and if I wake up and they're here, I'll make sure you regret it."

Again, that brief flare of pain he had no right to feel. How long had he wished his father would show him a sliver of softness? Any type of warmer emotion? Instead, he'd traded those feelings for becoming a drill sergeant with his boys, the total opposite of the way Mom had been. Not that he wanted to think of her anymore. It did no good except scrape against raw wounds. Caleb wasn't a martyr, so he stuffed that shit back down for another lifetime.

"Whatever, old man. Save the fight for the surgery."

They were interrupted when the Dr. Wang came in with an easy smile. "Okay, gentlemen, this is it. We gotta wheel him into surgery. Say your good-byes."

Caleb froze and stared into his father's familiar face. Took in the sharp, roughened features, leathery skin, bushy silver brows. Those brown eyes still held a fierce spark of life. In that moment, Caleb decided to take a chance. If something happened in surgery, he didn't want to regret it for the rest of his life.

He leaned down to kiss his father on the cheek.

Christian slapped him back with a growl. "Cut it out. Grow some balls. I'll see you later."

The tiny touch of emotion flickered out and left a cold, empty vastness inside his belly. So stupid. He felt so stupid. "Sure. Good luck, Dad."

"Don't need no damn luck. Make sure you do what I say. I don't want to see your brothers."

They were the last words Caleb heard as his father was wheeled into a surgery that took over five hours to perform.

The next morning Christian Pierce was dead.

And then the nightmare really began.

On behalf of 1001 Dark Nights,

Liz Berry and M.J. Rose would like to thank ~

Steve Berry
Doug Scofield
Kim Guidroz
Jillian Stein
InkSlinger PR
Dan Slater
Asha Hossain
Chris Graham
Pamela Jamison
Jessica Johns
Dylan Stockton
Richard Blake
BookTrib After Dark
The Dinner Party Show
and Simon Lipskar

CPSIA information can be obtained at www.ICGtesting.com
Printed in the USA
LVOW07s0540070616

491424LV00001B/289/P